ANNOYING ORANGE™

AUTOGRAPH?

HOW CAN I SIGN YOUR BOOK? I DON'T EVEN HAVE HANDS!

PAPERCUTZ™

ANNOYING ORANGE

AND OTHER GRAPHIC NOVELS AVAILABLE FROM PAPERCUTZ™

ANNOYING ORANGE
MY NAME IS ORANGE, SECRET AGENT ORANGE!
SCOTT SHAW! MIKE KAZALEH
PAPERCUTZ

ANNOYING ORANGE
Graphic Novel #1
"Secret Agent Orange"

PAPERCUTZ SLICES
AN ALL-NEW UNAUTHORIZED PARODY
Harry Potty
AND THE DEATHLY BORING
STEFAN PETRUCHA
RICK PARKER
PAPERCUTZ

PAPERCUTZ SLICES
Graphic Novel #1
"Harry Potty and the Deathly Boring"

PAPERCUTZ SLICES
AN ALL-NEW UNAUTHORIZED PARODY
breaking down
MAIA KINNEY-PETRUCHA & STEFAN PETRUCHA
RICK PARKER
PAPERCUTZ

PAPERCUTZ SLICES
Graphic Novel #2
"breaking down"

PAPERCUTZ SLICES
AN ALL-NEW UNAUTHORIZED PARODY
PERCY JERKSON
& THE OVOLACTOVEGETARIANS
PAPERCUTZ

PAPERCUTZ SLICES
Graphic Novel #3
"Percy Jerkson & The Ovolactovegetarians"

PAPERCUTZ SLICES
AN ALL-NEW UNAUTHORIZED PARODY
THE HUNGER PAINS
Stefan PETRUCHA
Rick PARKER
PAPERCUTZ

PAPERCUTZ SLICES
Graphic Novel #4
"The Hunger Pains"

ANNOYING ORANGE and PAPERCUTZ SLICES graphic novels, the print editions, are still available at booksellers everywhere.

Or order directly from Papercutz. ANNOYING ORANGE and PAPERCUTZ SLICES are available in paperback for $6.99 each; in hardcover for $10.99 each, please add $4.00 for postage and handling for the first book, and add $1.00 for each additional book. Make check payable to NBM Publishing.

Send to: Papercutz, 160 Broadway, Suite 700, East Wing, New York, NY 10038

Or call 800-886-1223 between 9-5 EST, M-F. Visa, MC, and AmEx accepted.

www.papercutz.com

ANNOYING ORANGE and PAPERCUTZ SLICES graphic novels are also available digitally wherever e-books are sold.

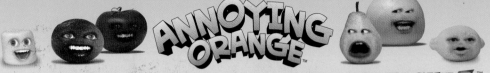

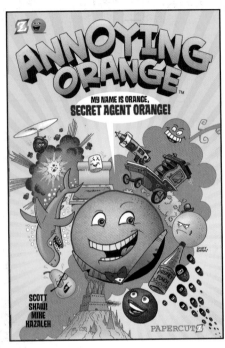

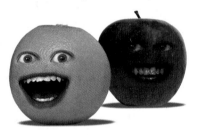

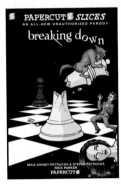

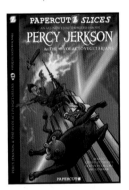

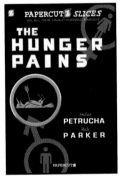

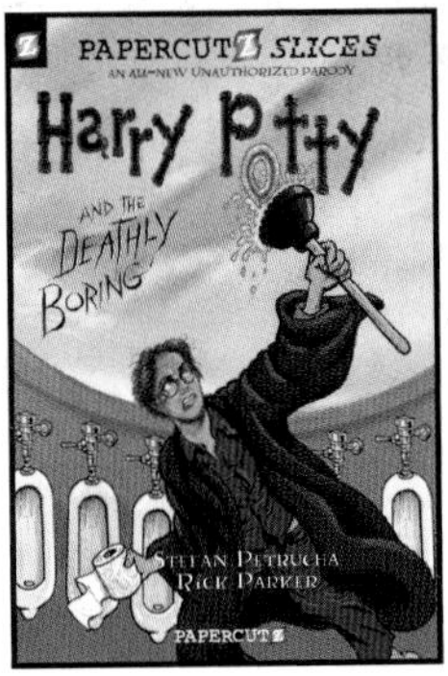

ANNOYING ORANGE ™

SECRET AGENT ORANGE

HEY! I'M A *GRAPHIC NOVEL!*

Annoying Orange is created by DANE BOEDIGHEIMER

MIKE KAZALEH – Writer & Artist

SCOTT SHAW! – Writer & Artist

LAURIE E. SMITH – Colorist

SCOTT SHAW! – Cover Artist

JAYJAY JACKSON – Cover Colorist

PAPERCUTZ™

NEW YORK

1 "Secret Agent Orange"
"The Adventures of Marshmallow,"
"A Bedtime Story,"
"Bowling for Hollers,"
"Exciting Scenes from Our Next Graphic Novel,"
"Nerville, the Ladies' Man,"
"One Fine Day in the Produce Section,"
"Plum's Day Out,"
"The Salad Days of Grandpa Lemon,"
and "The Snow Contest"
Mike Kazaleh – Writer & Artist
Laurie E. Smith – Colorist
Tom Orzechowski – Letterer
"Grapefinger"
Scott Shaw! – Writer & Artist
Jayjay Jackson – Laurie E. Smith
Tom Orzechowski – Letterer
Janice Chiang – Letterer
Scott Shaw! – Cover Artist
Jayjay Jackson – Cover Colorist

Special thanks to: Gary Binkow, Tim Blankley, Dane Boedigheimer, Kristy Fagan,
Spencer Grove, Teresa Harris, Reza Izad, Debra Joester, Polina Rey, Jess Richardson
Design & Production – Nelson Design Group, LLC
Director of Marketing – Jesse Post
Associate Editor – Michael Petranek
Jim Salicrup
Editor-in-Chief

ISBN: 978-1-59707-361-5 paperback edition
ISBN: 978-1-59707-362-2 hardcover edition

Printed in Canada
December 2012 by Friesens Printing
1 Printers Way
Altona, MB R0G 0B0

Distributed by Macmillan
First Printing

MEET THE FRUIT...

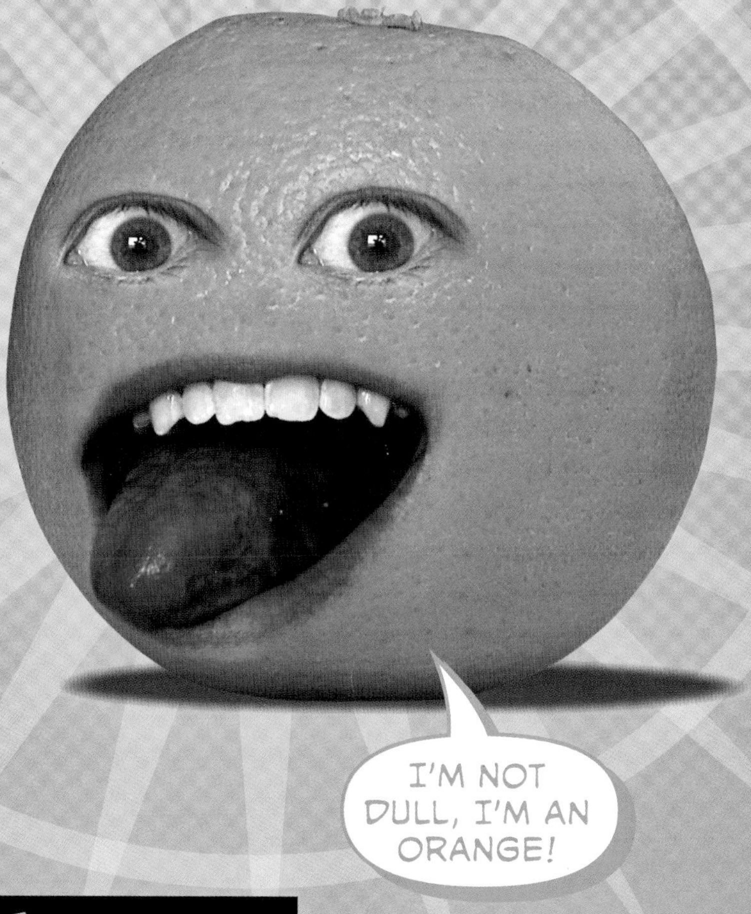
I'M NOT DULL, I'M AN ORANGE!

ORANGE

He's cute. He's sweet (sort of). He's Annoying. He's an Orange! To some, he's the king of comedy, the prince of puns, the earl of irritation! And to others, he's just a royal pun in the bottom. Call him what you will, but don't call him an apple. He hates that!

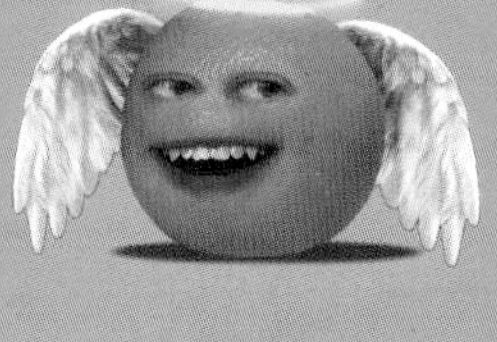

PEAR

Just like Orange, Pear is loaded with Vitamin C, but that's pretty much where similarities end. Despite their differences, Pear and Orange are best buds, a great "pair" of friends. Whenever Orange is around, Pear knows something interesting will happen.

LEAVE ME OUT OF THIS!

MIDGET APPLE

THAT'S *LITTLE* APPLE!

The only apple in Orange's entourage is Midget Apple. He constantly corrects others regarding his name, insisting that he's Little Apple (although Small and Tiny are also acceptable), but even he can't deny that he is indeed small. Midget Apple's best friend is Marshmallow. What Midget, er, ah, Little Apple lacks in size, he more than makes up for in laughs and loyalty.

PASSION FRUIT

Like the name implies, Passion Fruit is full of life! She's cheerful and calm, though she can get angry with Orange when he talks about others in an Annoying way. She's not just a hottie, but a smartie as well! Although she does have a little crush on Orange, and in turn she is the object of his affections! Too bad she doesn't know that!

HEY! WATCH THE MERCHANDISE, BUDDY!

MARSHMALLOW

RAINBOWS ARE DELICIOUS!

Marshmallow is a real sweetheart, and it has nothing to do with sugar or gelatin! Marshmallow is made with sunshine, rainbows, and fun! There's even a rumor that Marshmallow's part unicorn. YAY! Danger never seems to bother Marshmallow. Even when roasted Marshmallow only felt "gooey"! Marshmallow truly is sweetness incarnate... YAY!

GRANDPA LEMON

Grandpa Lemon is by far the oldest fruit around. He's also the sleepiest. At odd times he will drift off and… zzzzzzz… fall asleep. Grandpa Lemon is a bit hard of hearing at times and forgetful. By falling asleep and forgetting Orange's jokes, he's capable of annoying Orange! Despite his narcolepsy, being sliced, juiced, made into lemonade, he's little worse for wear. Which only proves that any way you slice him, Grandpa Lemon is here to stay!

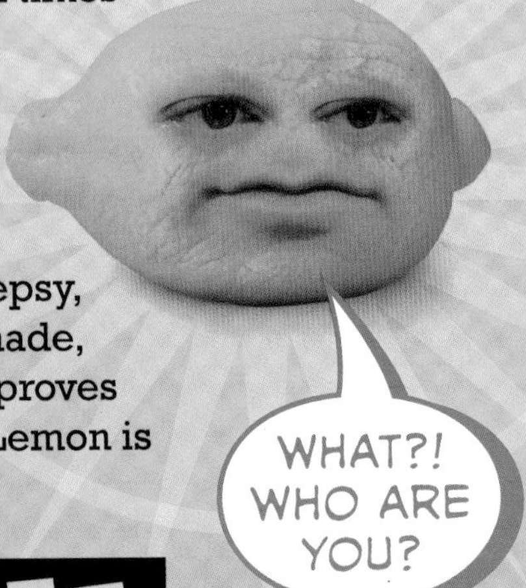
WHAT?! WHO ARE YOU?

GRAPEFRUIT

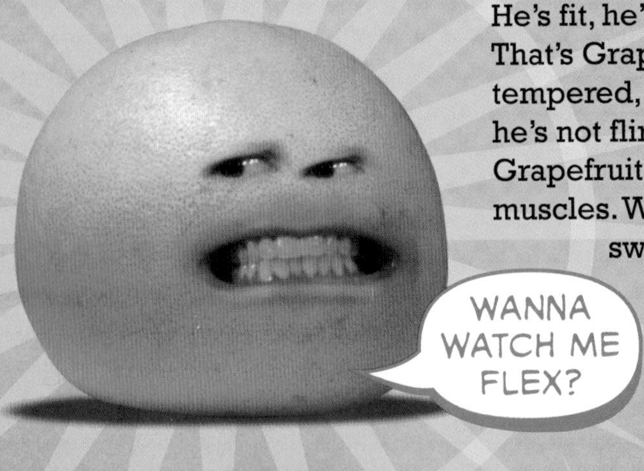
WANNA WATCH ME FLEX?

He's fit, he's firm, he's flexing! That's Grapefruit—a cranky, bad-tempered, tightfisted fruit. When he's not flirting with female fruits, Grapefruit is boasting about his muscles. When he's not breaking a sweat, he's breaking your bones! And if he's not breaking bones, he's breaking hearts! OH!

APPLE

A friend of Orange's but he's constantly annoyed by Orange's jokes, puns, and stories. He often loses his temper when Orange refuses to be quiet. Apple is not a big fan of knives.

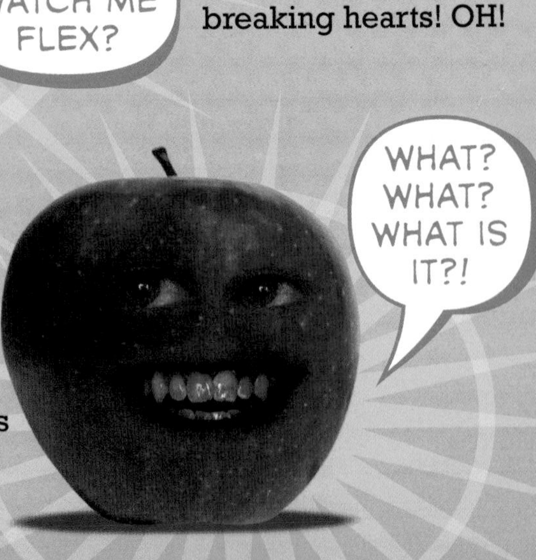
WHAT? WHAT? WHAT IS IT?!

ONE FINE DAY IN THE PRODUCE SECTION

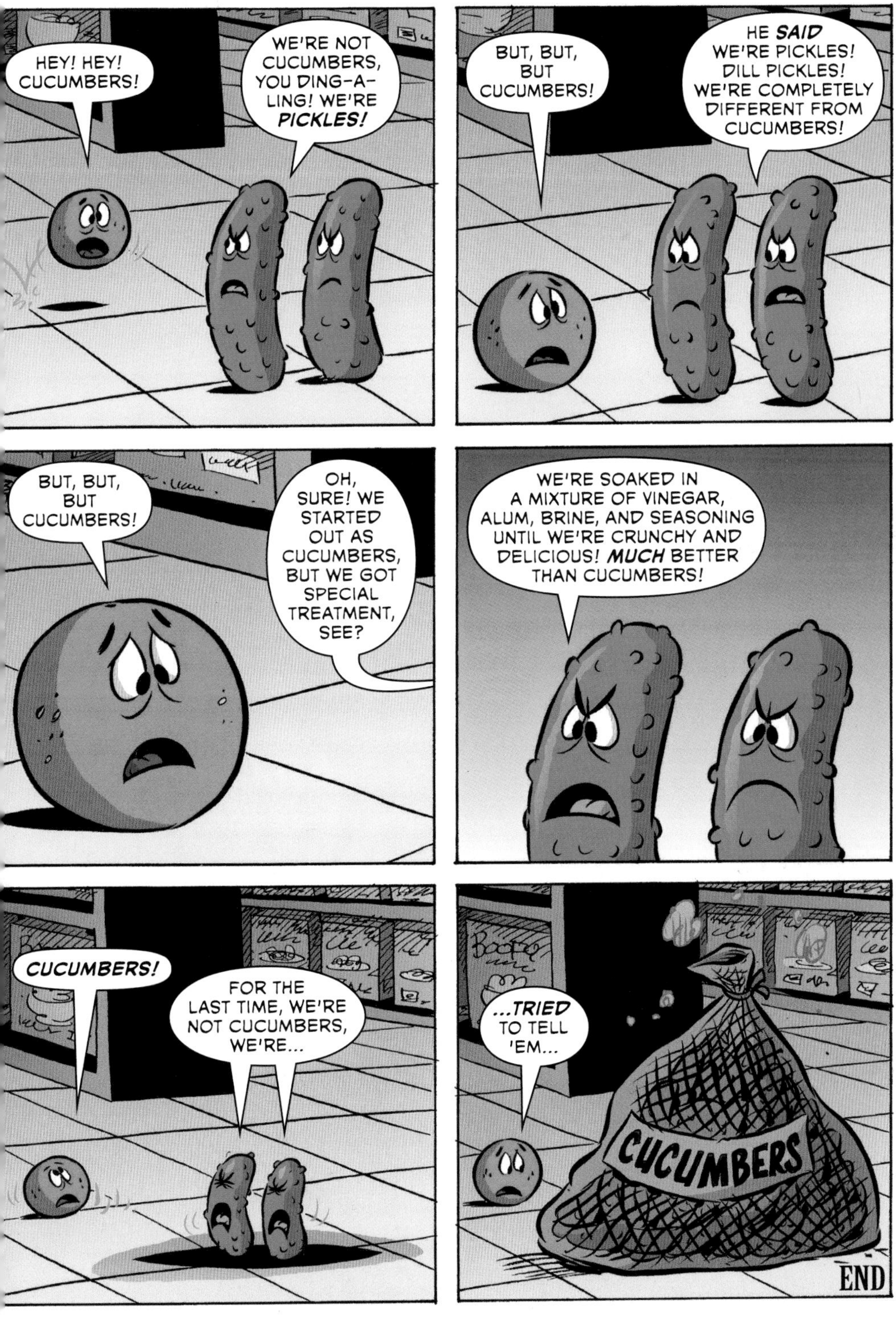
HEY! HEY! CUCUMBERS!
WE'RE NOT CUCUMBERS, YOU DING-A-LING! WE'RE *PICKLES!*
BUT, BUT, BUT CUCUMBERS!
HE *SAID* WE'RE PICKLES! DILL PICKLES! WE'RE COMPLETELY DIFFERENT FROM CUCUMBERS!
BUT, BUT, BUT CUCUMBERS!
OH, SURE! WE STARTED OUT AS CUCUMBERS, BUT WE GOT SPECIAL TREATMENT, SEE?
WE'RE SOAKED IN A MIXTURE OF VINEGAR, ALUM, BRINE, AND SEASONING UNTIL WE'RE CRUNCHY AND DELICIOUS! *MUCH* BETTER THAN CUCUMBERS!
CUCUMBERS!
FOR THE LAST TIME, WE'RE NOT CUCUMBERS, WE'RE...
...TRIED TO TELL 'EM...
CUCUMBERS
END

Nerville, The Ladies' Man

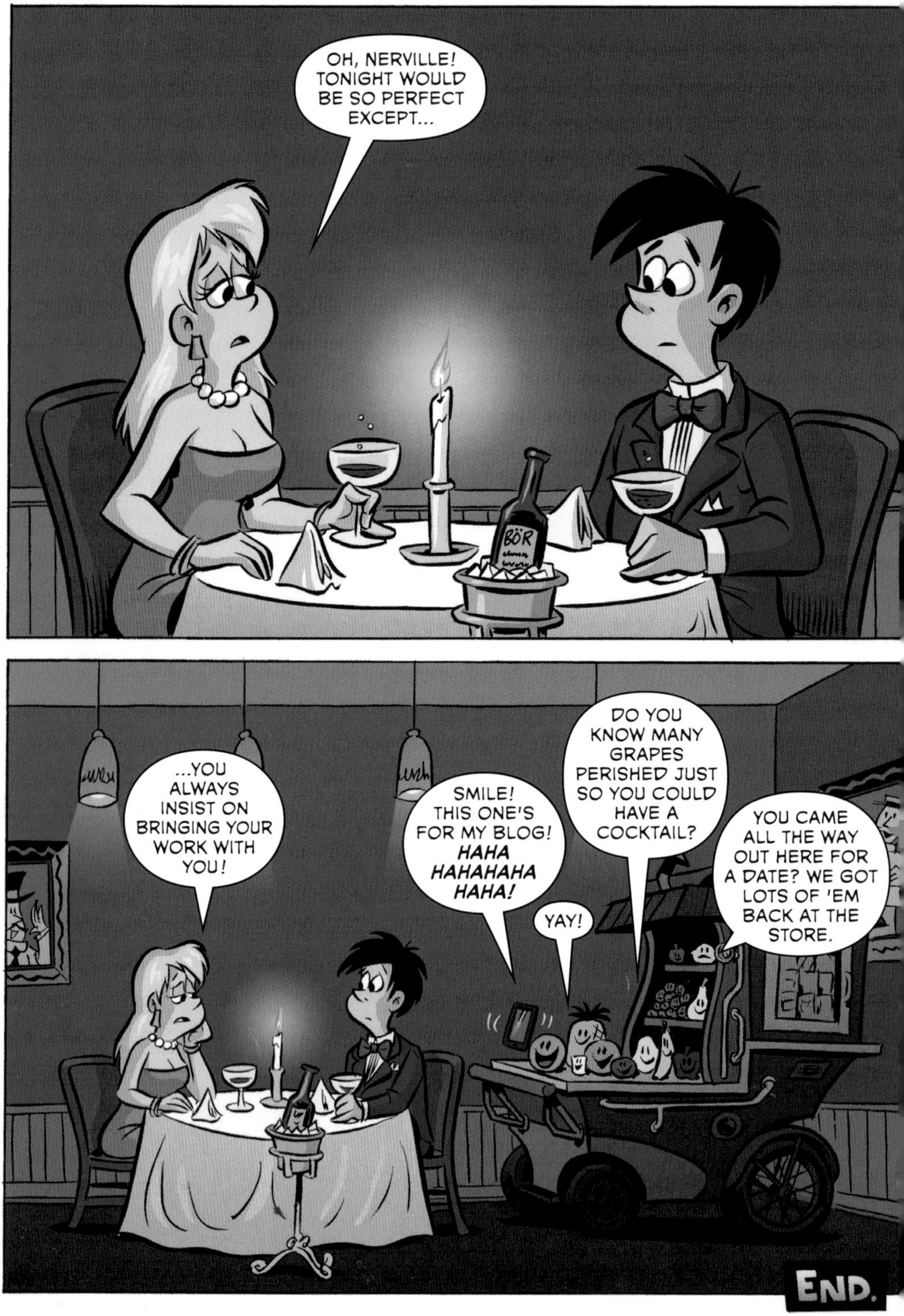
OH, NERVILLE! TONIGHT WOULD BE SO PERFECT EXCEPT...
BÖR
...YOU ALWAYS INSIST ON BRINGING YOUR WORK WITH YOU!
SMILE! THIS ONE'S FOR MY BLOG! *HAHA HAHAHAHA HAHA!*
YAY!
DO YOU KNOW MANY GRAPES PERISHED JUST SO YOU COULD HAVE A COCKTAIL?
YOU CAME ALL THE WAY OUT HERE FOR A DATE? WE GOT LOTS OF 'EM BACK AT THE STORE.
END.

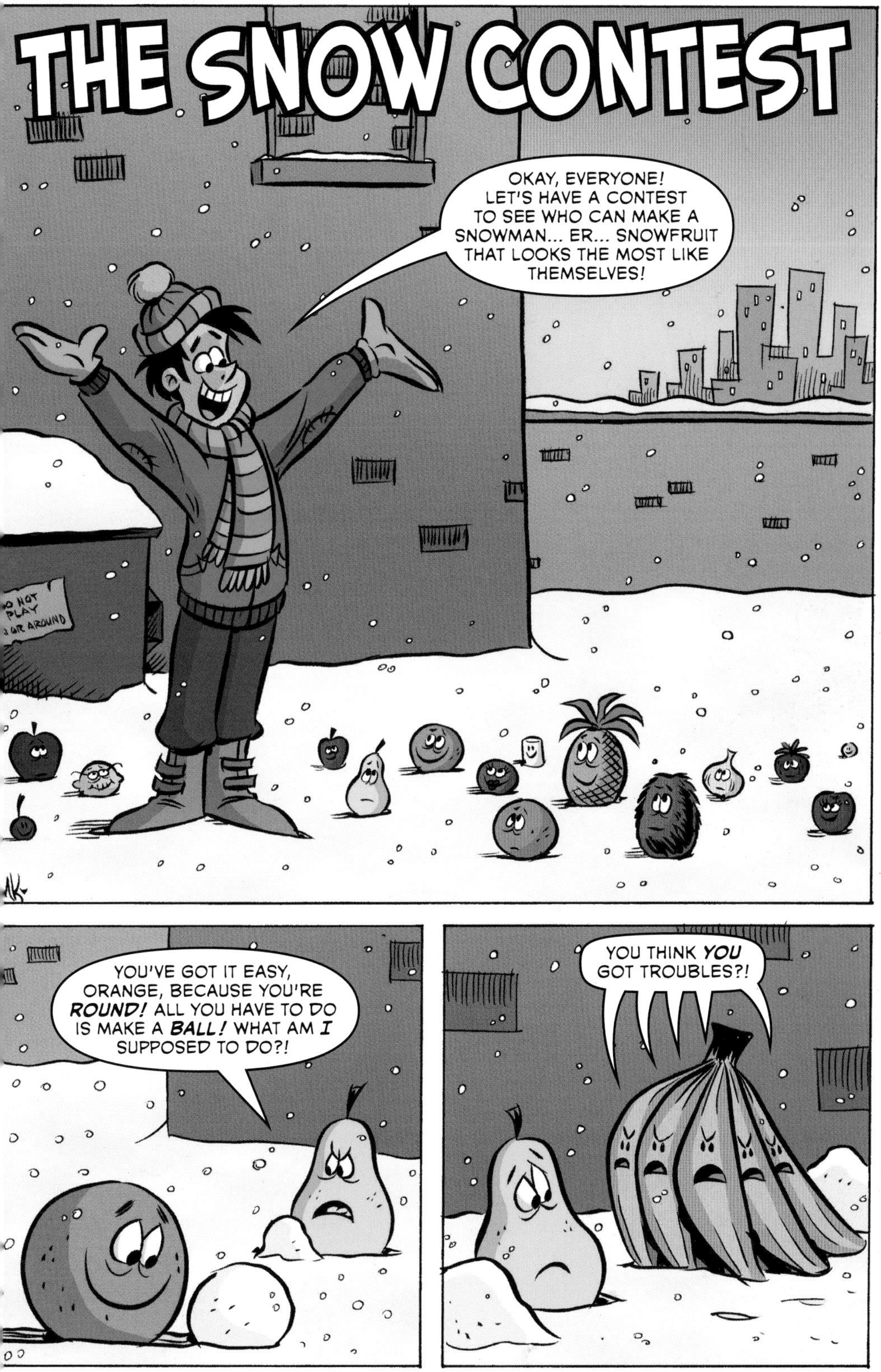
THE SNOW CONTEST
OKAY, EVERYONE! LET'S HAVE A CONTEST TO SEE WHO CAN MAKE A SNOWMAN... ER... SNOWFRUIT THAT LOOKS THE MOST LIKE THEMSELVES!
YOU'VE GOT IT EASY, ORANGE, BECAUSE YOU'RE *ROUND!* ALL YOU HAVE TO DO IS MAKE A *BALL!* WHAT AM *I* SUPPOSED TO DO?!
YOU THINK *YOU* GOT TROUBLES?!

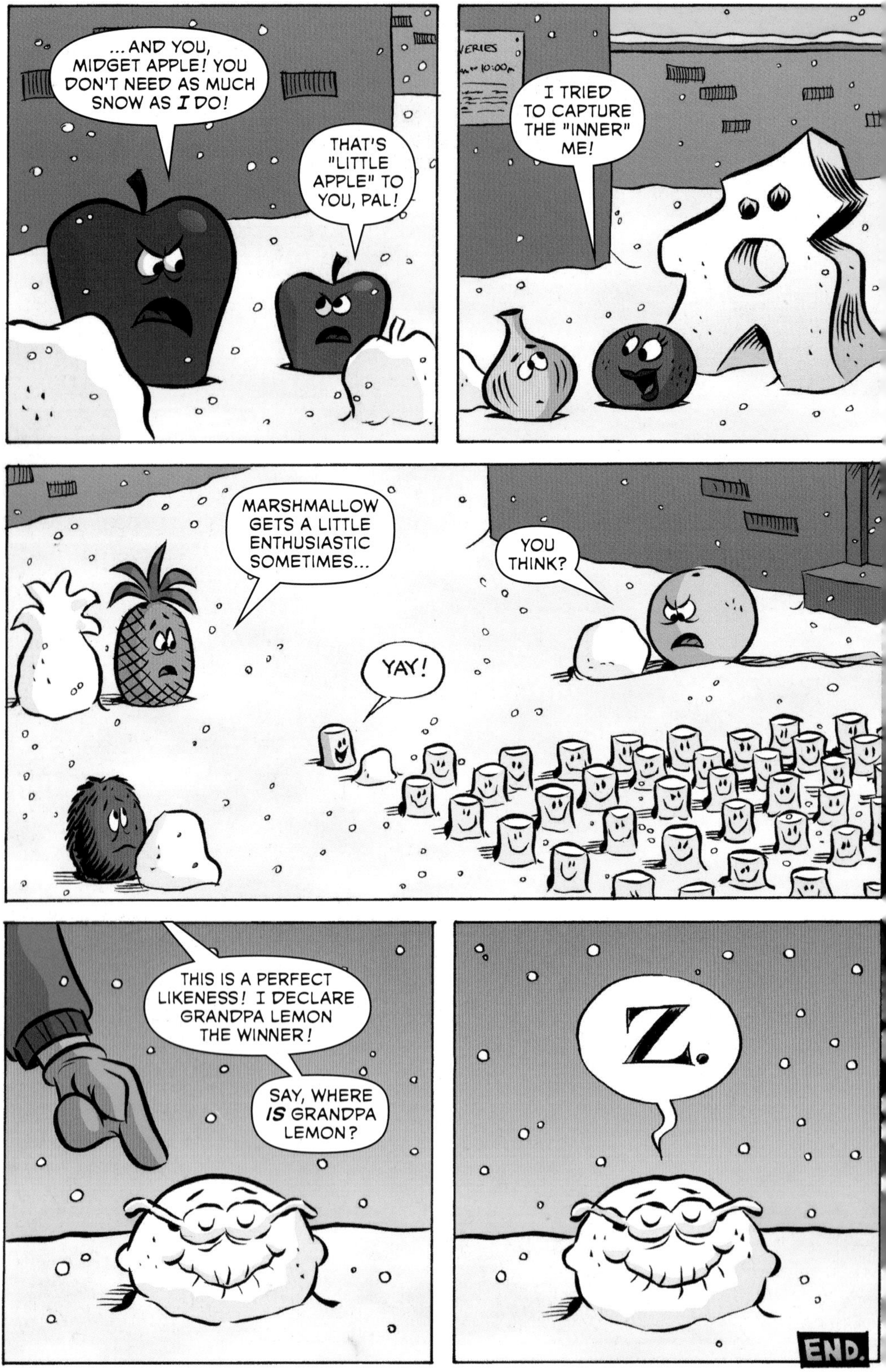
...AND YOU, MIDGET APPLE! YOU DON'T NEED AS MUCH SNOW AS *I* DO!
THAT'S "LITTLE APPLE" TO YOU, PAL!
I TRIED TO CAPTURE THE "INNER" ME!
MARSHMALLOW GETS A LITTLE ENTHUSIASTIC SOMETIMES...
YOU THINK?
YAY!
THIS IS A PERFECT LIKENESS! I DECLARE GRANDPA LEMON THE WINNER!
SAY, WHERE ***IS*** GRANDPA LEMON?
Z.
END.

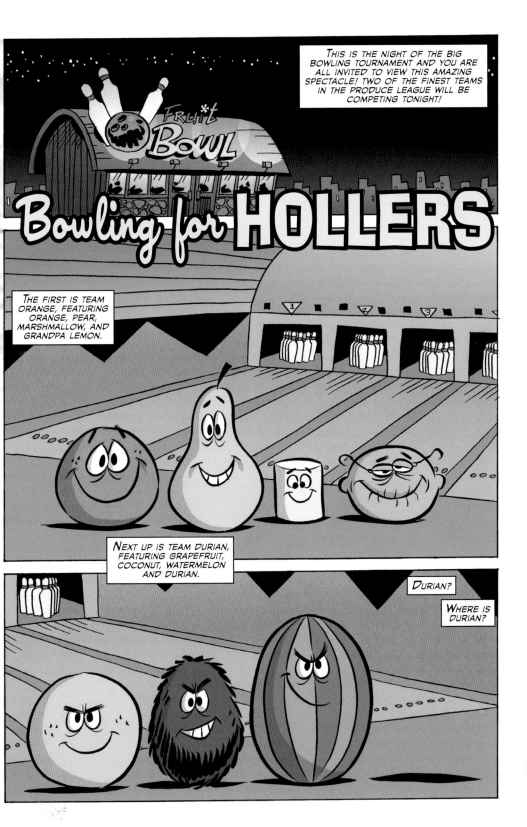

THIS IS THE NIGHT OF THE BIG BOWLING TOURNAMENT AND YOU ARE ALL INVITED TO VIEW THIS AMAZING SPECTACLE! TWO OF THE FINEST TEAMS IN THE PRODUCE LEAGUE WILL BE COMPETING TONIGHT!

Fruit Bowl

Bowling for HOLLERS

THE FIRST IS TEAM ORANGE, FEATURING ORANGE, PEAR, MARSHMALLOW, AND GRANDPA LEMON.

NEXT UP IS TEAM DURIAN, FEATURING GRAPEFRUIT, COCONUT, WATERMELON AND DURIAN.

DURIAN?

WHERE IS DURIAN?

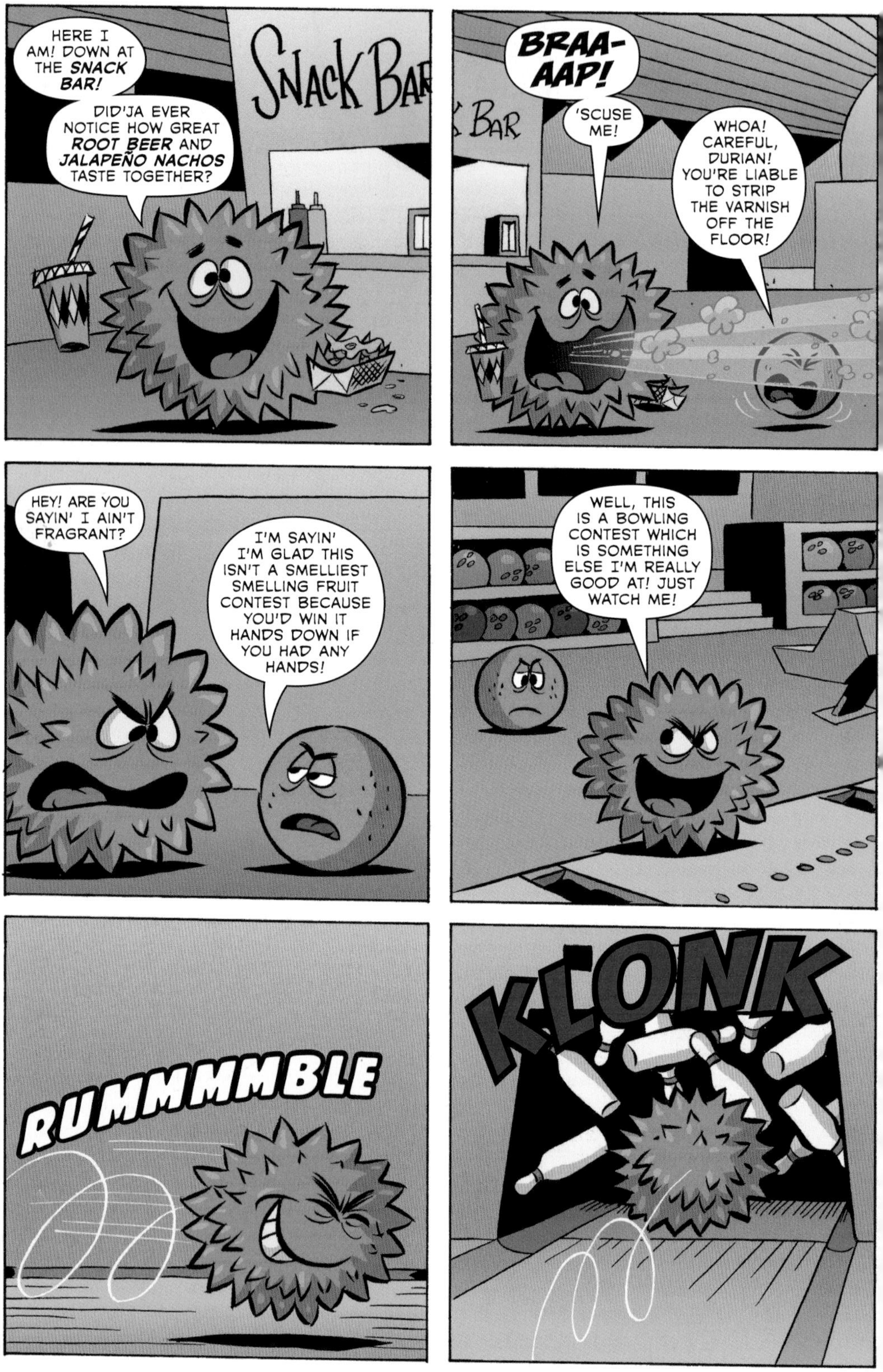
HERE I AM! DOWN AT THE SNACK BAR!
DID'JA EVER NOTICE HOW GREAT ROOT BEER AND JALAPEÑO NACHOS TASTE TOGETHER?
SNACK BAR
BRAA-AAP!
'SCUSE ME!
WHOA! CAREFUL, DURIAN! YOU'RE LIABLE TO STRIP THE VARNISH OFF THE FLOOR!
HEY! ARE YOU SAYIN' I AIN'T FRAGRANT?
I'M SAYIN' I'M GLAD THIS ISN'T A SMELLIEST SMELLING FRUIT CONTEST BECAUSE YOU'D WIN IT HANDS DOWN IF YOU HAD ANY HANDS!
WELL, THIS IS A BOWLING CONTEST WHICH IS SOMETHING ELSE I'M REALLY GOOD AT! JUST WATCH ME!
RUMMMMBLE
KLONK

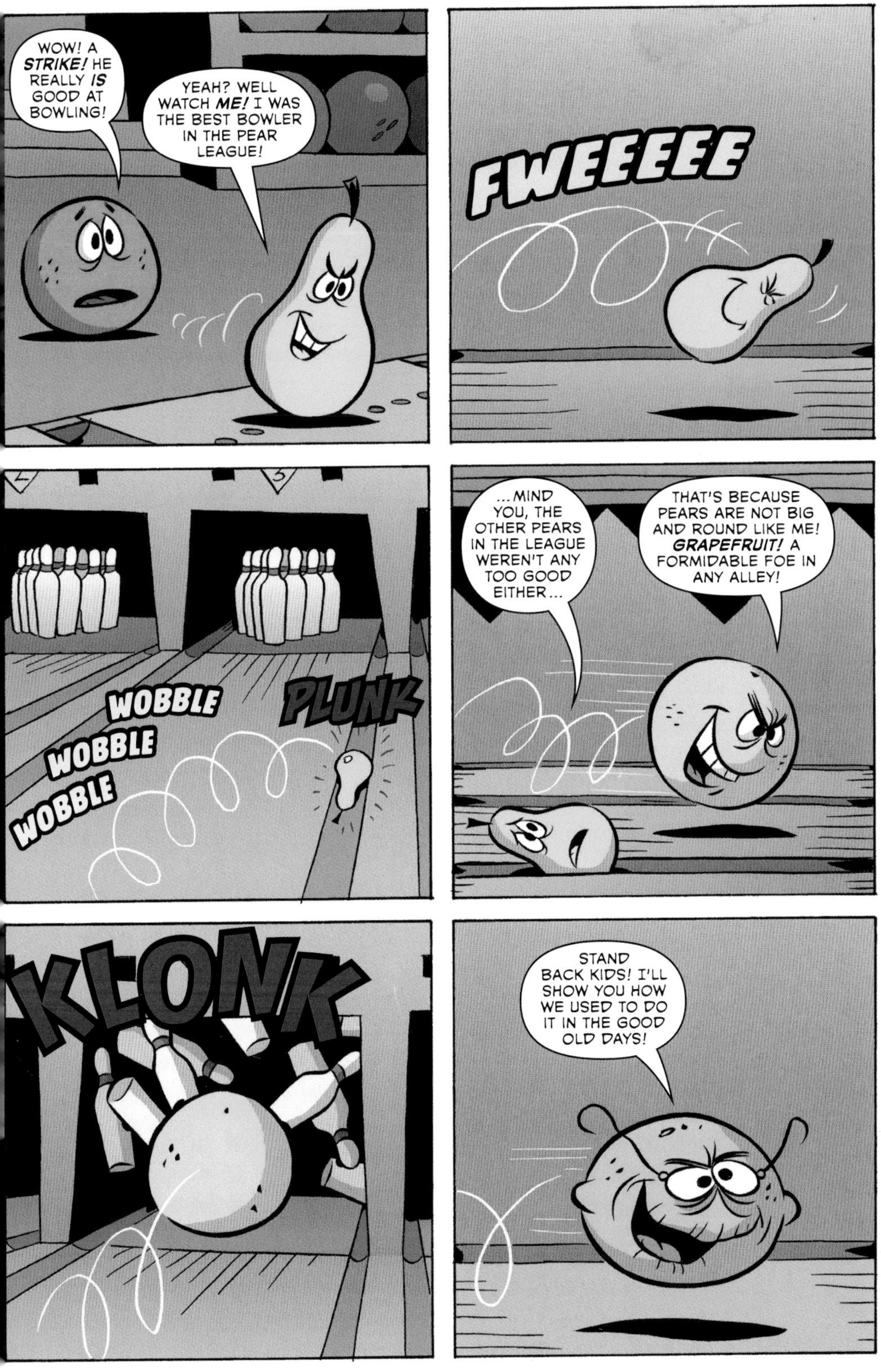
WOW! A STRIKE! HE REALLY IS GOOD AT BOWLING!
YEAH? WELL WATCH ME! I WAS THE BEST BOWLER IN THE PEAR LEAGUE!
FWEEEEE
WOBBLE
WOBBLE
WOBBLE
PLUNK
...MIND YOU, THE OTHER PEARS IN THE LEAGUE WEREN'T ANY TOO GOOD EITHER...
THAT'S BECAUSE PEARS ARE NOT BIG AND ROUND LIKE ME! GRAPEFRUIT! A FORMIDABLE FOE IN ANY ALLEY!
KLONK
STAND BACK KIDS! I'LL SHOW YOU HOW WE USED TO DO IT IN THE GOOD OLD DAYS!

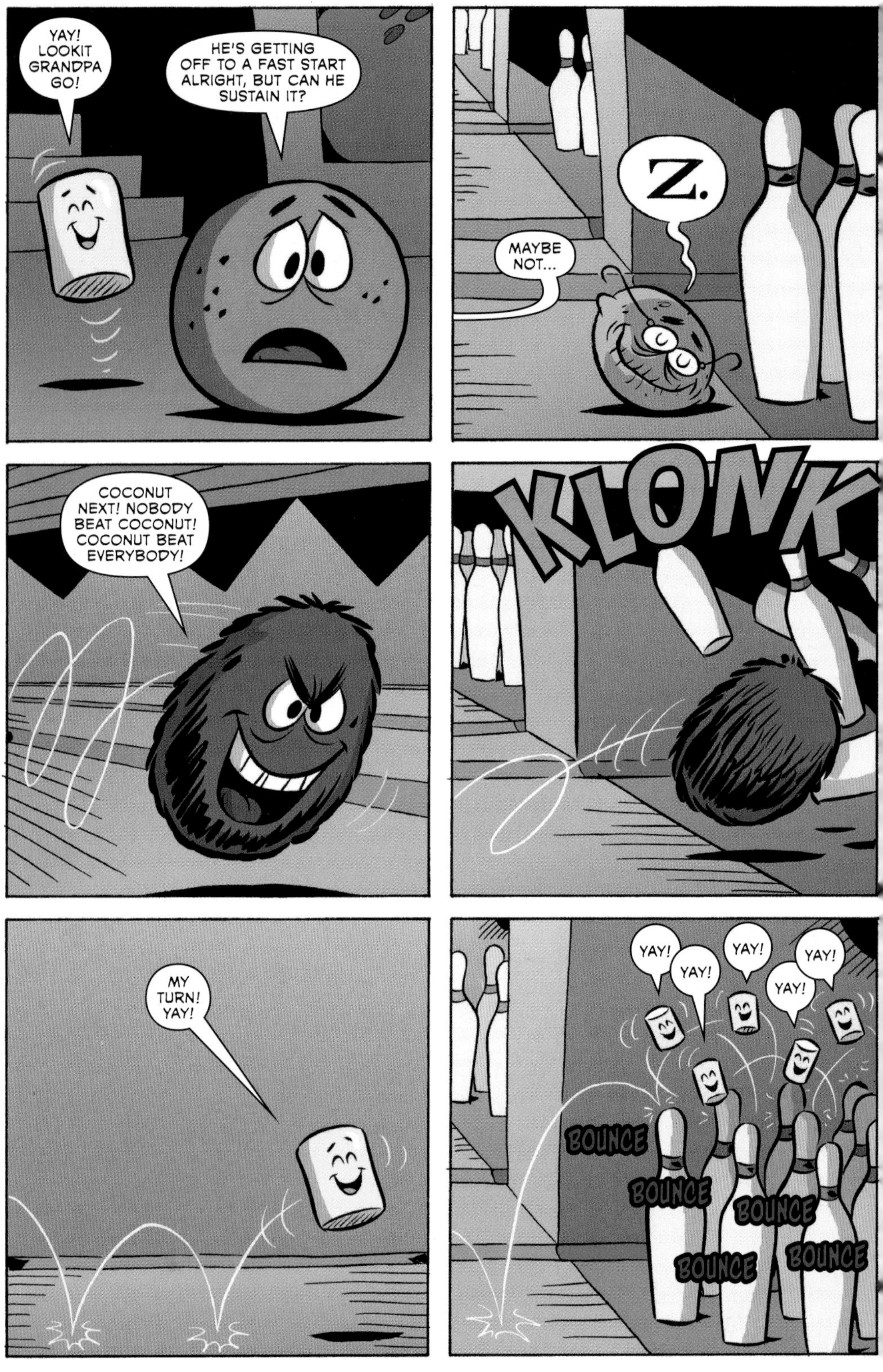
YAY! LOOKIT GRANDPA GO!
HE'S GETTING OFF TO A FAST START ALRIGHT, BUT CAN HE SUSTAIN IT?
Z.
MAYBE NOT...
COCONUT NEXT! NOBODY BEAT COCONUT! COCONUT BEAT EVERYBODY!
KLONK
MY TURN! YAY!
YAY!
YAY!
YAY!
YAY!
YAY!
BOUNCE
BOUNCE
BOUNCE
BOUNCE
BOUNCE

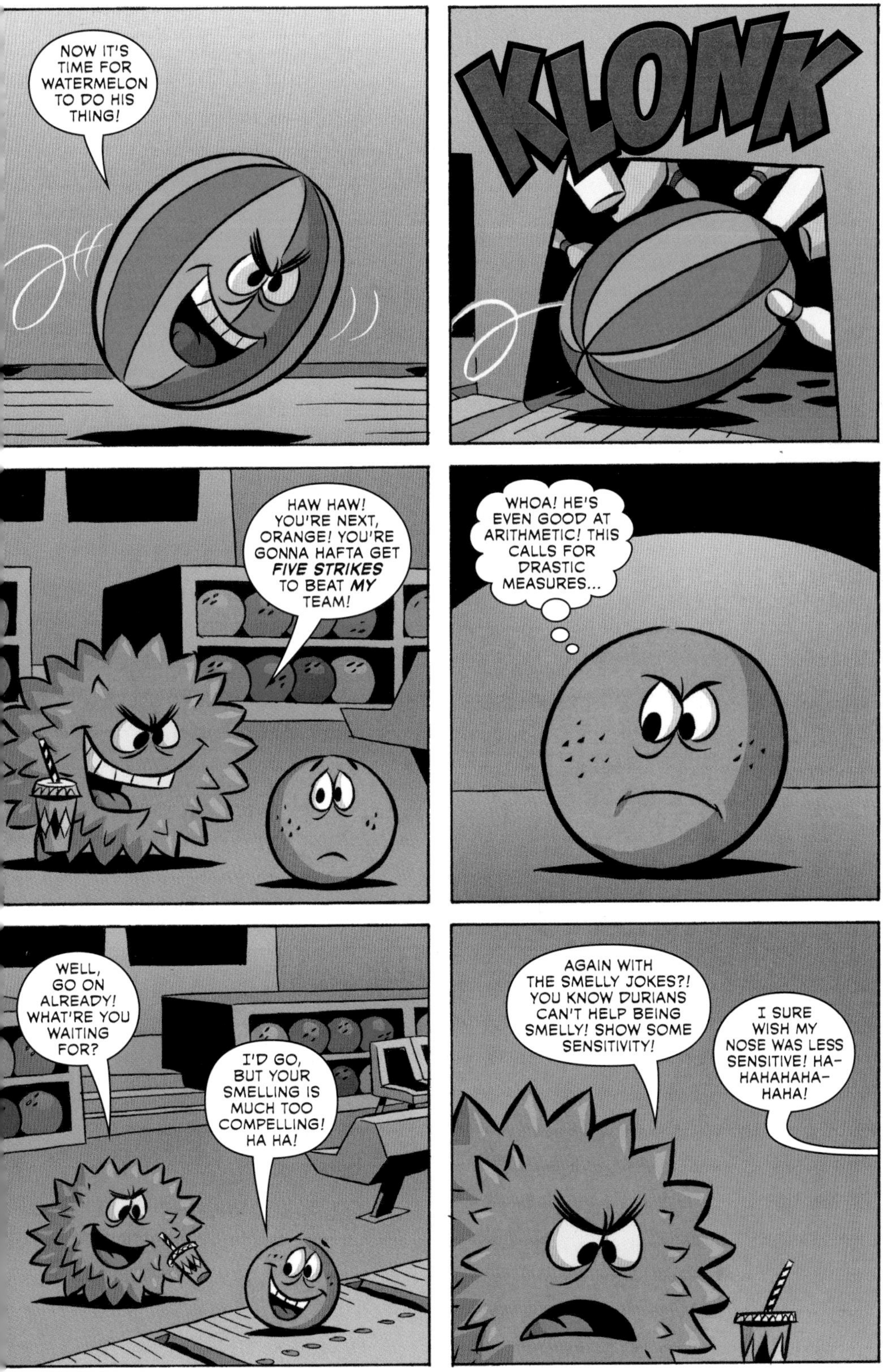
NOW IT'S TIME FOR WATERMELON TO DO HIS THING!
KLONK
HAW HAW! YOU'RE NEXT, ORANGE! YOU'RE GONNA HAFTA GET **FIVE STRIKES** TO BEAT **MY** TEAM!
WHOA! HE'S EVEN GOOD AT ARITHMETIC! THIS CALLS FOR DRASTIC MEASURES...
WELL, GO ON ALREADY! WHAT'RE YOU WAITING FOR?
I'D GO, BUT YOUR SMELLING IS MUCH TOO COMPELLING! HA HA!
AGAIN WITH THE SMELLY JOKES?! YOU KNOW DURIANS CAN'T HELP BEING SMELLY! SHOW SOME SENSITIVITY!
I SURE WISH MY NOSE WAS LESS SENSITIVE! HA-HAHAHAHA-HAHA!

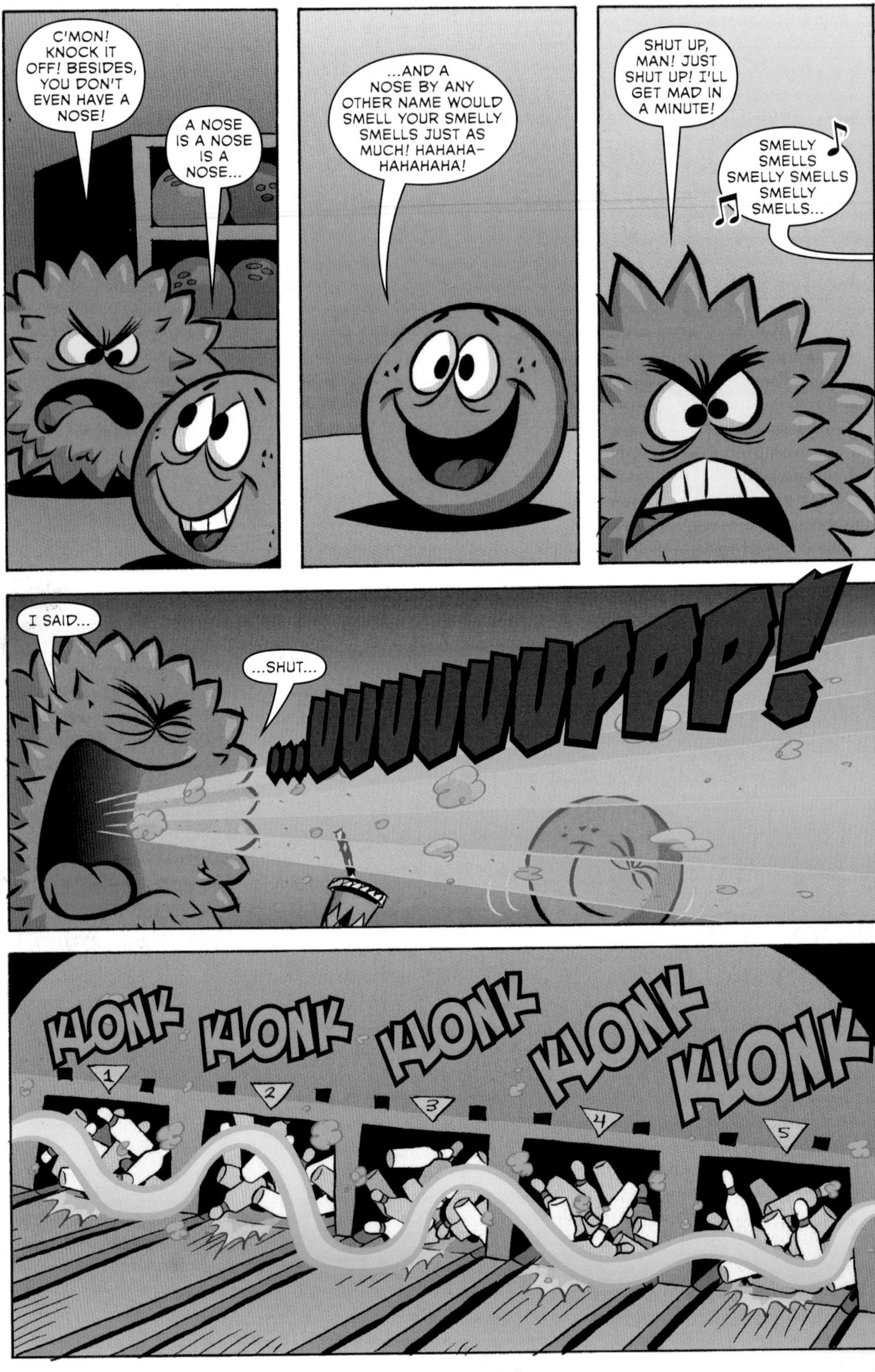
C'MON! KNOCK IT OFF! BESIDES, YOU DON'T EVEN HAVE A NOSE!
A NOSE IS A NOSE IS A NOSE...
...AND A NOSE BY ANY OTHER NAME WOULD SMELL YOUR SMELLY SMELLS JUST AS MUCH! HAHAHA-HAHAHAHA!
SHUT UP, MAN! JUST SHUT UP! I'LL GET MAD IN A MINUTE!
SMELLY SMELLS SMELLY SMELLS SMELLY SMELLS...
I SAID...
...SHUT...
...UUUUUUUPPP!
KLONK
KLONK
KLONK
KLONK
KLONK
1
2
3
4
5

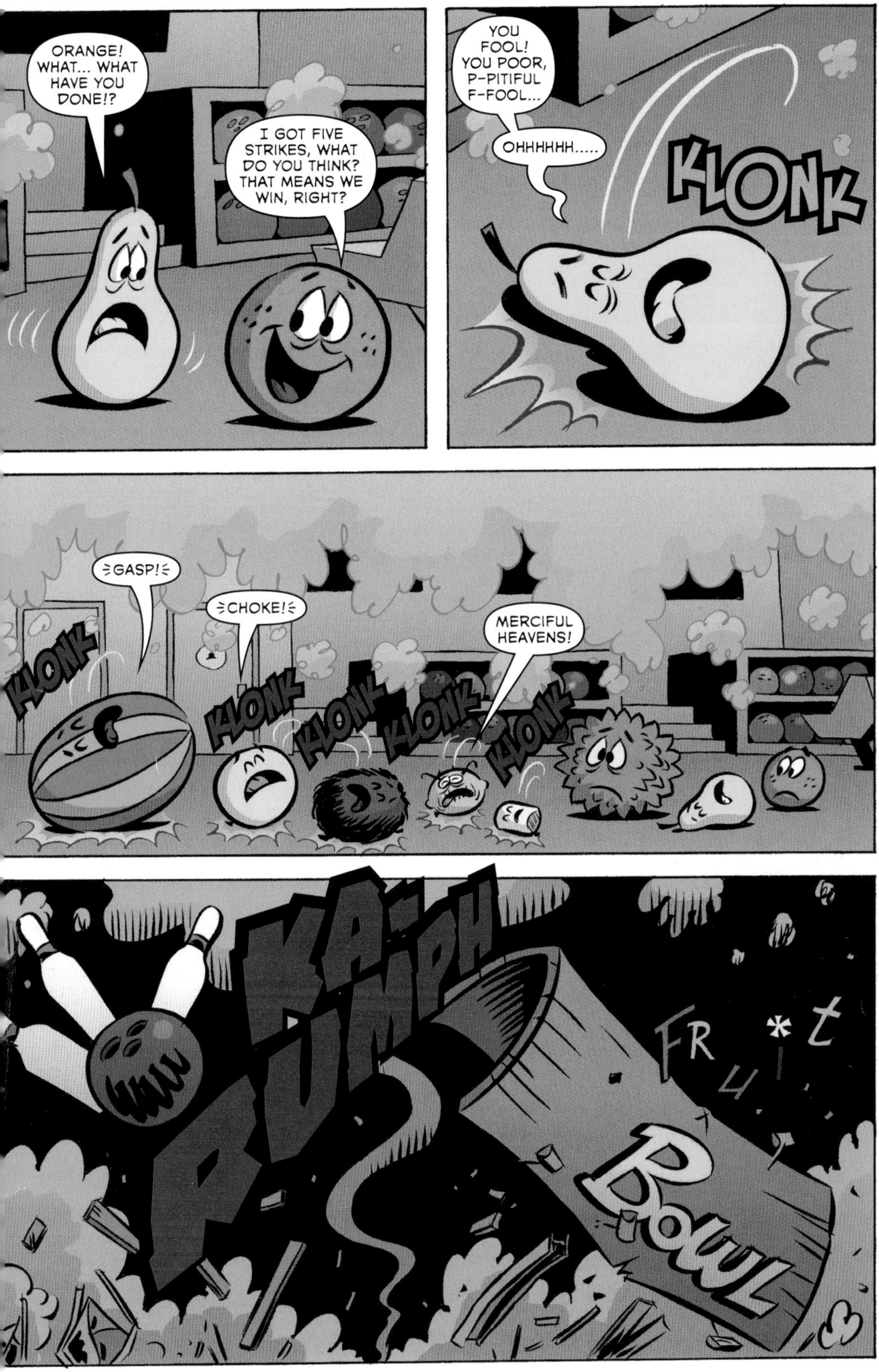
ORANGE! WHAT... WHAT HAVE YOU DONE!?
I GOT FIVE STRIKES, WHAT DO YOU THINK? THAT MEANS WE WIN, RIGHT?
YOU FOOL! YOU POOR, P-PITIFUL F-FOOL...
OHHHHHH.....
KLONK
GASP!
KLONK
CHOKE!
KLONK
KLONK
KLONK
MERCIFUL HEAVENS!
KLONK
KA-PUMPH
FRUIT
BOWL

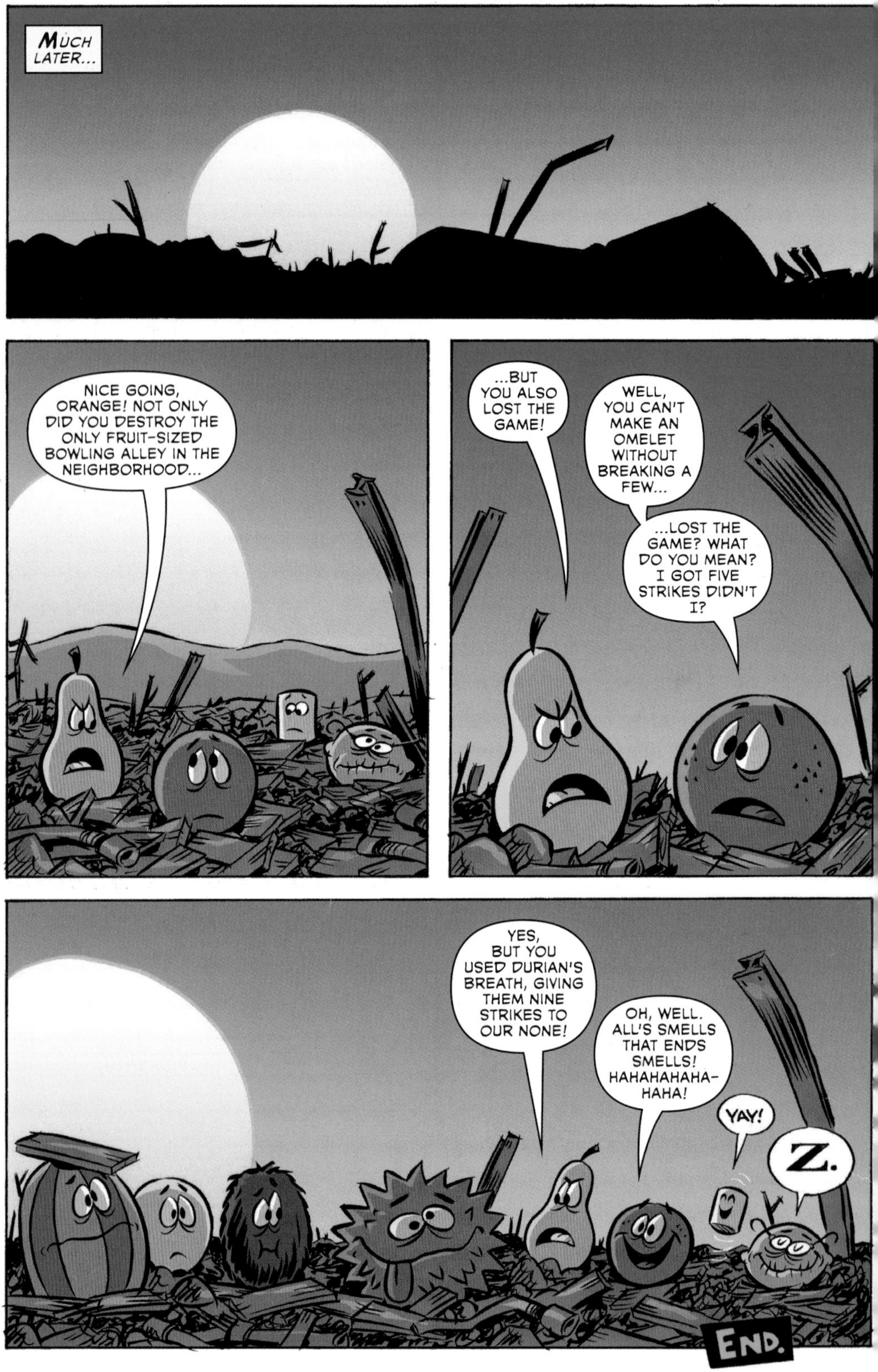
MUCH LATER...
NICE GOING, ORANGE! NOT ONLY DID YOU DESTROY THE ONLY FRUIT-SIZED BOWLING ALLEY IN THE NEIGHBORHOOD...
...BUT YOU ALSO LOST THE GAME!
WELL, YOU CAN'T MAKE AN OMELET WITHOUT BREAKING A FEW...
...LOST THE GAME? WHAT DO YOU MEAN? I GOT FIVE STRIKES DIDN'T I?
YES, BUT YOU USED DURIAN'S BREATH, GIVING THEM NINE STRIKES TO OUR NONE!
OH, WELL. ALL'S SMELLS THAT ENDS SMELLS! HAHAHAHAHA-HAHA!
YAY!
Z.
END.

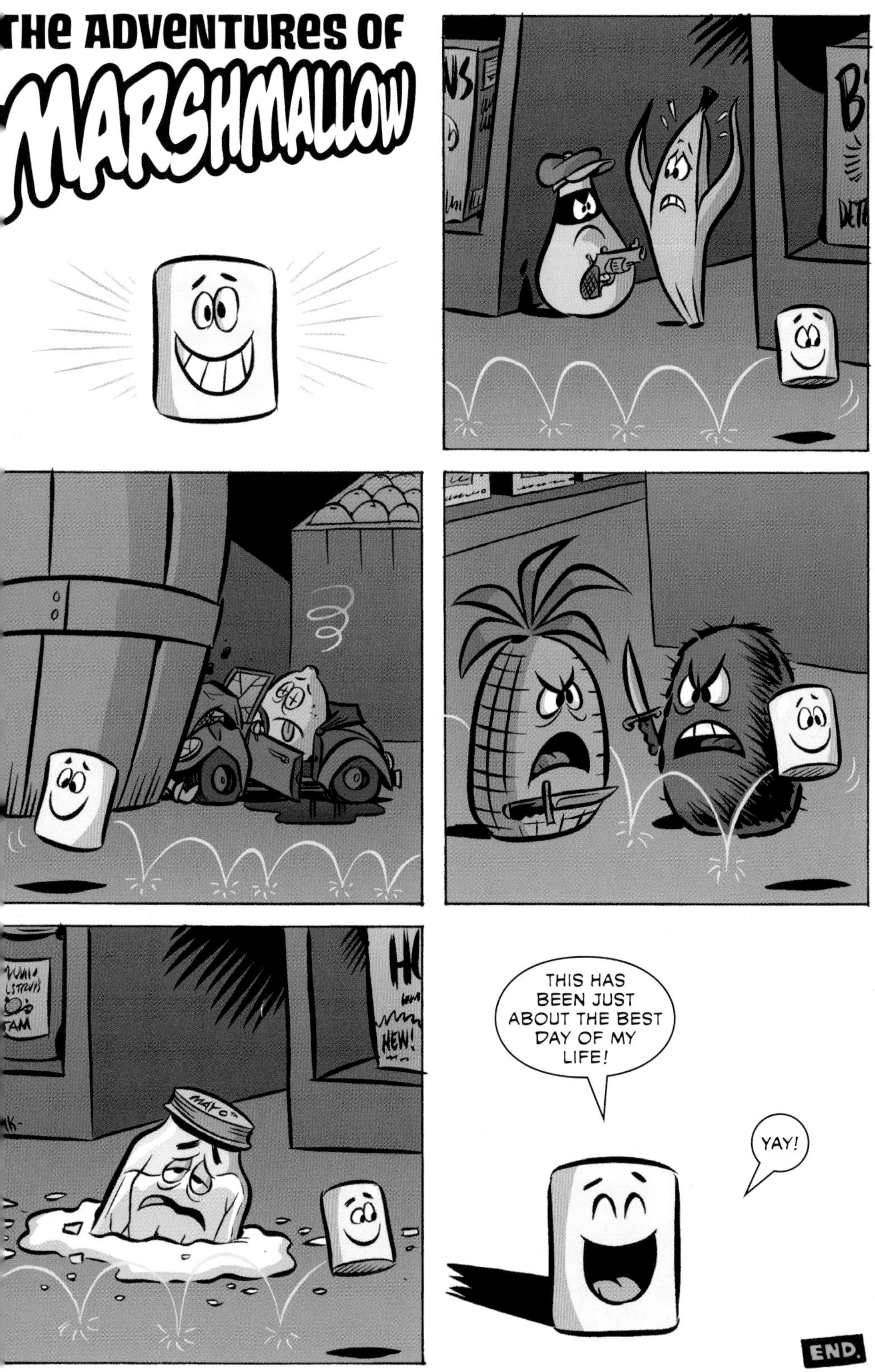
THE ADVENTURES OF
MARSHMALLOW
MAYO
NEW!
THIS HAS BEEN JUST ABOUT THE BEST DAY OF MY LIFE!
YAY!
END.

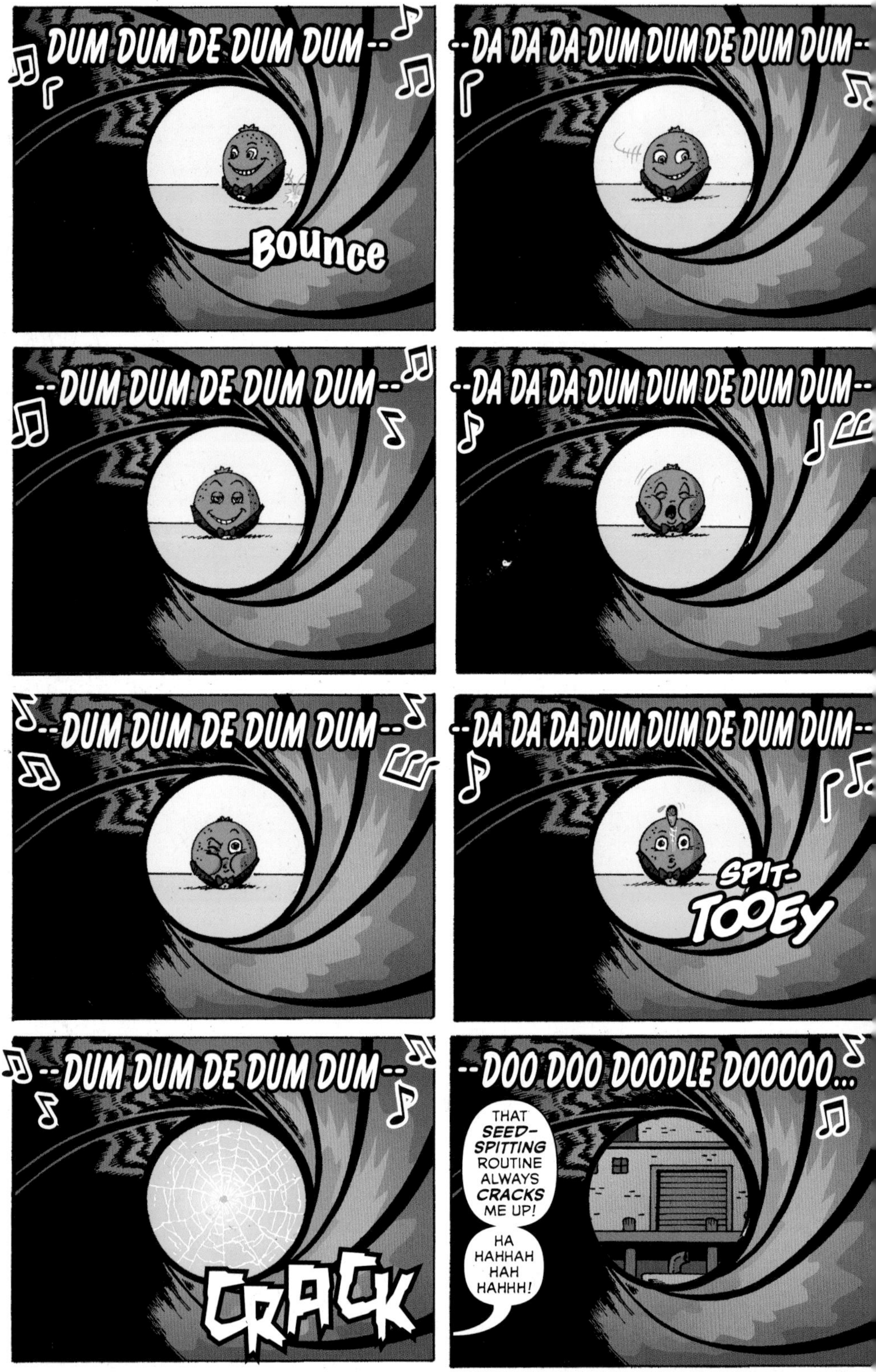
DUM DUM DE DUM DUM--
BOUNCE
--DA DA DA DUM DUM DE DUM DUM--
--DUM DUM DE DUM DUM--
--DA DA DA DUM DUM DE DUM DUM--
--DUM DUM DE DUM DUM--
--DA DA DA DUM DUM DE DUM DUM--
SPIT-TOOEY
--DUM DUM DE DUM DUM--
CRACK
--DOO DOO DOODLE DOOOOO...
THAT SEED-SPITTING ROUTINE ALWAYS CRACKS ME UP!
HA HAHHAH HAH HAHHH!

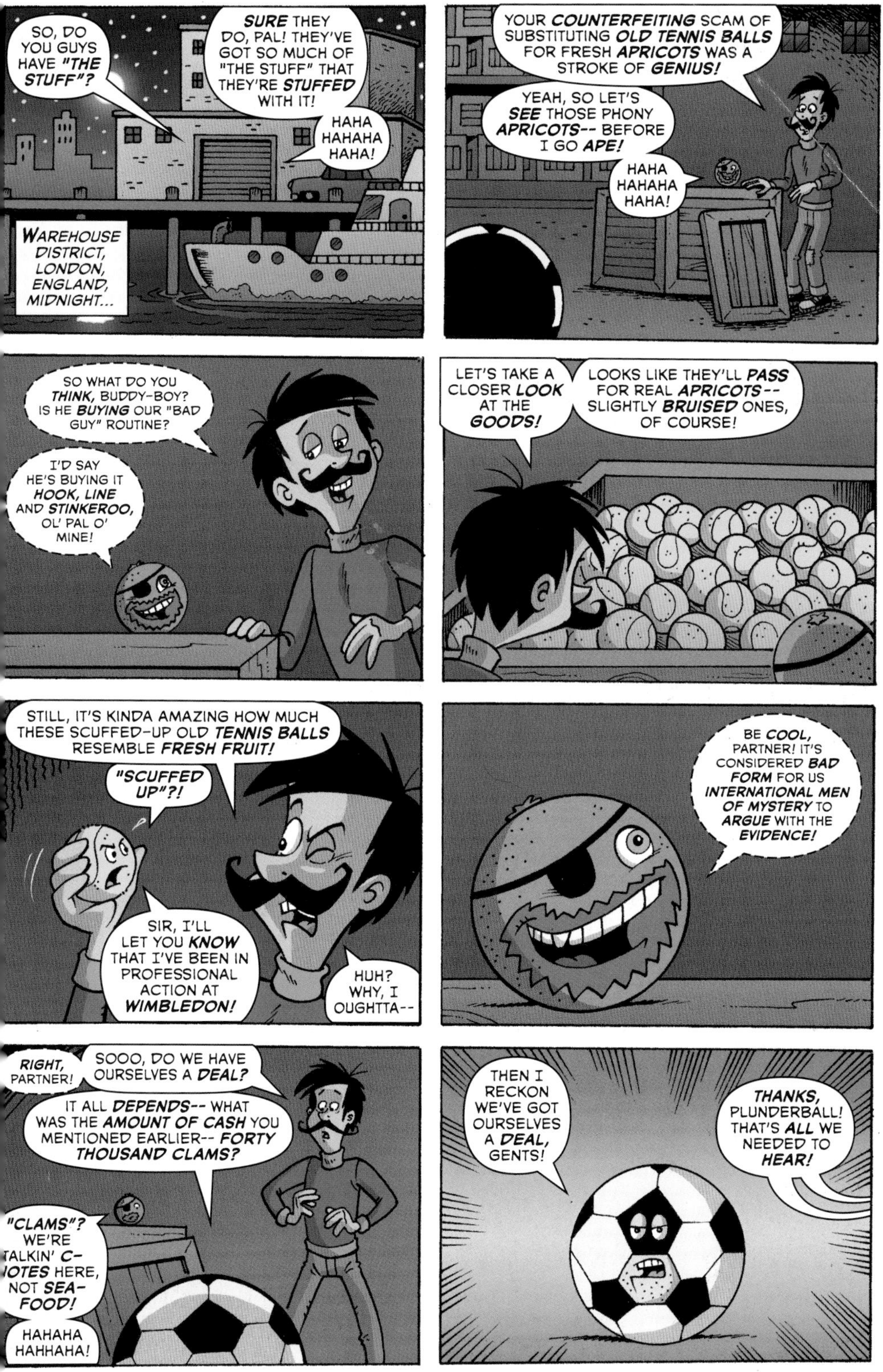
SO, DO YOU GUYS HAVE "THE STUFF"?
SURE THEY DO, PAL! THEY'VE GOT SO MUCH OF "THE STUFF" THAT THEY'RE STUFFED WITH IT!
HAHA HAHAHA HAHA!
WAREHOUSE DISTRICT, LONDON, ENGLAND, MIDNIGHT...
YOUR COUNTERFEITING SCAM OF SUBSTITUTING OLD TENNIS BALLS FOR FRESH APRICOTS WAS A STROKE OF GENIUS!
YEAH, SO LET'S SEE THOSE PHONY APRICOTS-- BEFORE I GO APE!
HAHA HAHAHA HAHA!
SO WHAT DO YOU THINK, BUDDY-BOY? IS HE BUYING OUR "BAD GUY" ROUTINE?
I'D SAY HE'S BUYING IT HOOK, LINE AND STINKEROO, OL' PAL O' MINE!
LET'S TAKE A CLOSER LOOK AT THE GOODS!
LOOKS LIKE THEY'LL PASS FOR REAL APRICOTS-- SLIGHTLY BRUISED ONES, OF COURSE!
STILL, IT'S KINDA AMAZING HOW MUCH THESE SCUFFED-UP OLD TENNIS BALLS RESEMBLE FRESH FRUIT!
"SCUFFED UP"?!
SIR, I'LL LET YOU KNOW THAT I'VE BEEN IN PROFESSIONAL ACTION AT WIMBLEDON!
HUH? WHY, I OUGHTTA--
BE COOL, PARTNER! IT'S CONSIDERED BAD FORM FOR US INTERNATIONAL MEN OF MYSTERY TO ARGUE WITH THE EVIDENCE!
RIGHT, PARTNER!
SOOO, DO WE HAVE OURSELVES A DEAL?
IT ALL DEPENDS-- WHAT WAS THE AMOUNT OF CASH YOU MENTIONED EARLIER-- FORTY THOUSAND CLAMS?
"CLAMS"? WE'RE TALKIN' C-NOTES HERE, NOT SEA-FOOD!
HAHAHA HAHHAHA!
THEN I RECKON WE'VE GOT OURSELVES A DEAL, GENTS!
THANKS, PLUNDERBALL! THAT'S ALL WE NEEDED TO HEAR!

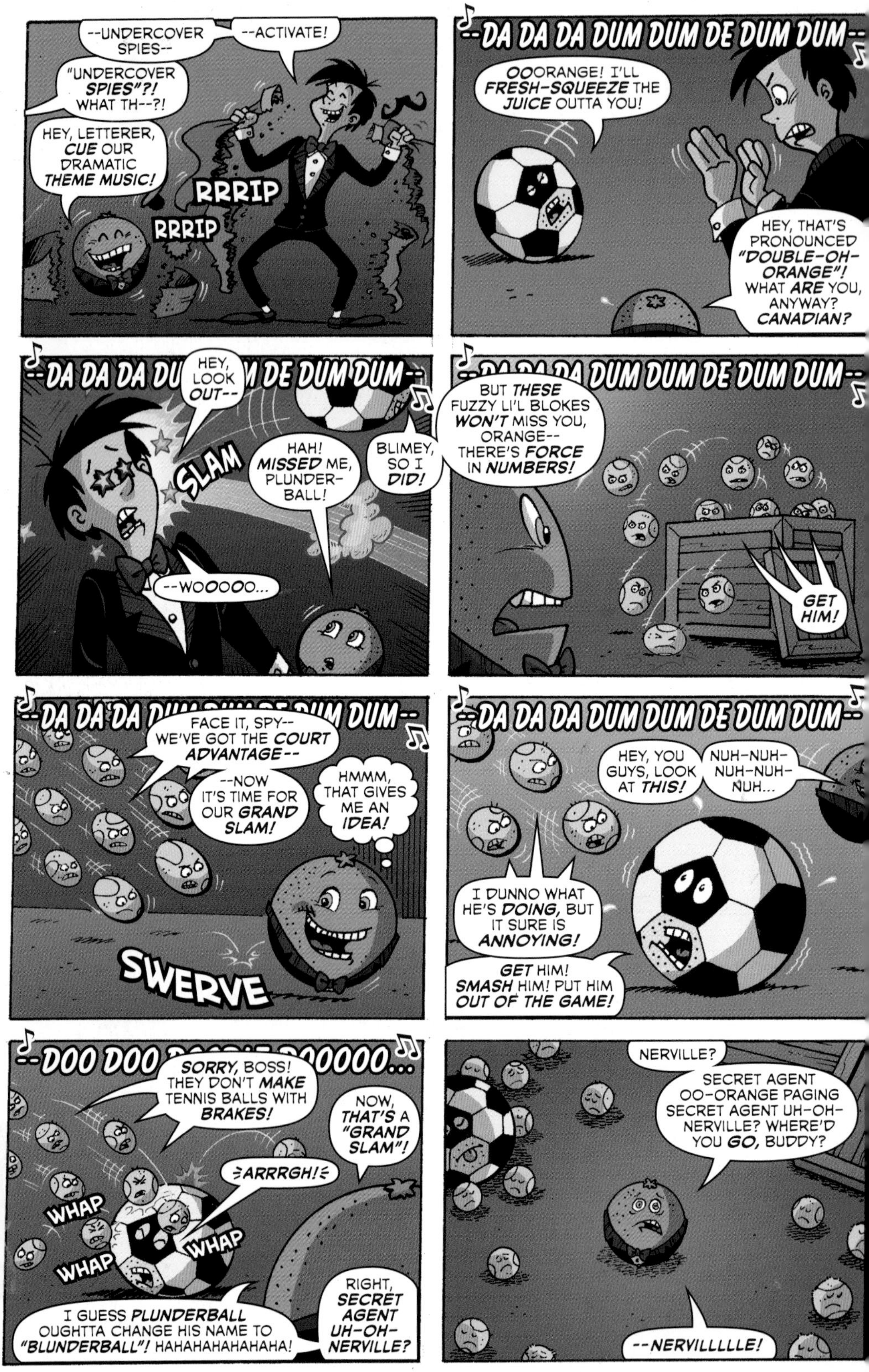
--UNDERCOVER SPIES--
--ACTIVATE!
"UNDERCOVER SPIES"?! WHAT TH--?!
HEY, LETTERER, CUE OUR DRAMATIC THEME MUSIC!
RRRIP
RRRIP
--DA DA DA DUM DUM DE DUM DUM--
OOORANGE! I'LL FRESH-SQUEEZE THE JUICE OUTTA YOU!
HEY, THAT'S PRONOUNCED "DOUBLE-OH-ORANGE"! WHAT ARE YOU, ANYWAY? CANADIAN?
HEY, LOOK OUT--
SLAM
HAH! MISSED ME, PLUNDER-BALL!
BLIMEY, SO I DID!
--WOOOOO...
DUM DUM DE DUM DUM--
BUT THESE FUZZY LI'L BLOKES WON'T MISS YOU, ORANGE-- THERE'S FORCE IN NUMBERS!
GET HIM!
FACE IT, SPY-- WE'VE GOT THE COURT ADVANTAGE--
--NOW IT'S TIME FOR OUR GRAND SLAM!
HMMM, THAT GIVES ME AN IDEA!
SWERVE
--DA DA DA DUM DUM DE DUM DUM--
HEY, YOU GUYS, LOOK AT THIS!
NUH-NUH-NUH-NUH-NUH...
I DUNNO WHAT HE'S DOING, BUT IT SURE IS ANNOYING!
GET HIM! SMASH HIM! PUT HIM OUT OF THE GAME!
--DOO DOO
OOOOOO...
SORRY, BOSS! THEY DON'T MAKE TENNIS BALLS WITH BRAKES!
NOW, THAT'S A "GRAND SLAM"!
ARRRGH!
WHAP
WHAP
WHAP
I GUESS PLUNDERBALL OUGHTTA CHANGE HIS NAME TO "BLUNDERBALL"! HAHAHAHAHAHAHA!
RIGHT, SECRET AGENT UH-OH-NERVILLE?
NERVILLE?
SECRET AGENT OO-ORANGE PAGING SECRET AGENT UH-OH-NERVILLE? WHERE'D YOU GO, BUDDY?
--NERVILLLLLE!

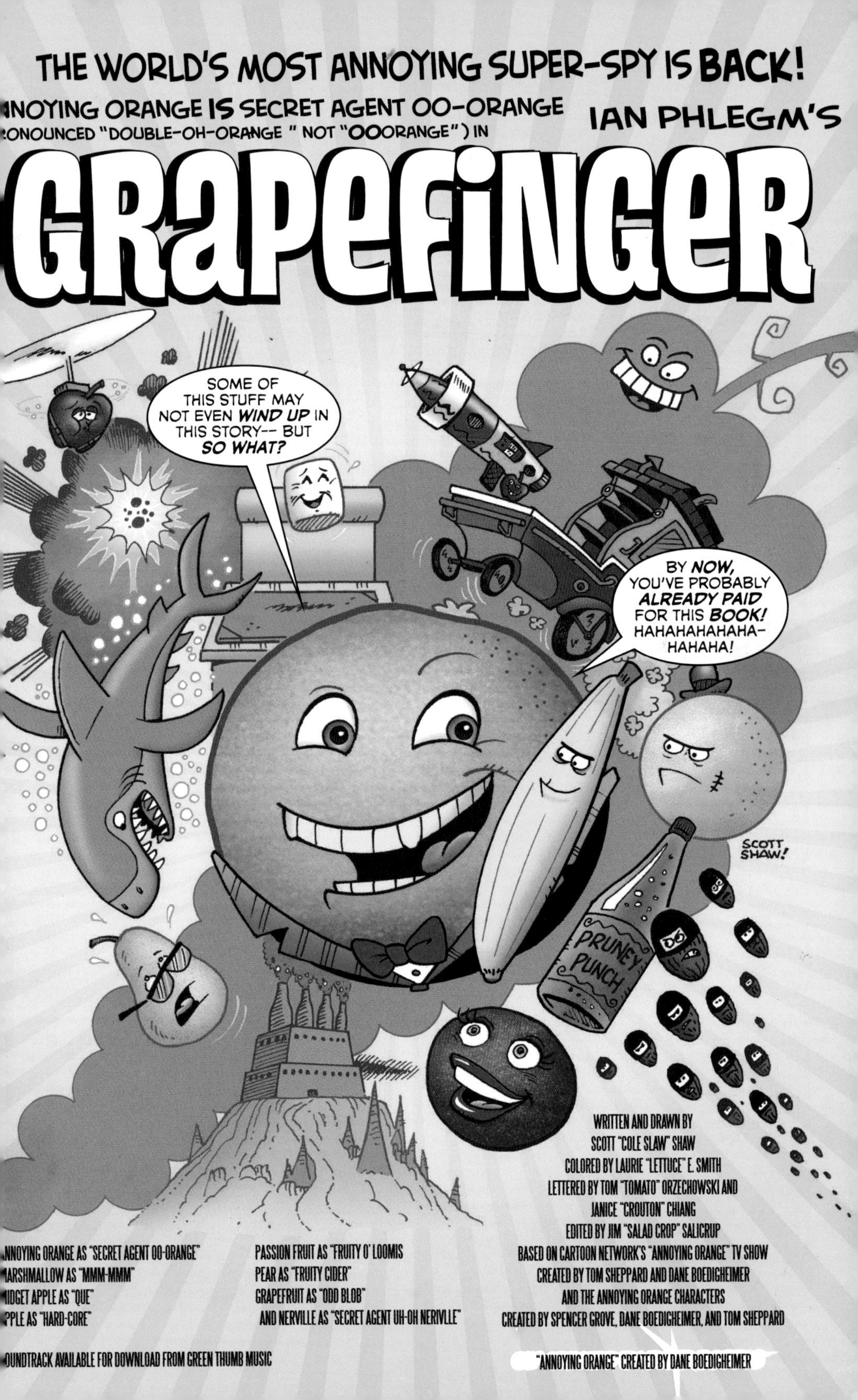
THE WORLD'S MOST ANNOYING SUPER-SPY IS BACK!
NNOYING ORANGE IS SECRET AGENT OO-ORANGE
RONOUNCED "DOUBLE-OH-ORANGE " NOT "OOORANGE") IN
IAN PHLEGM'S
GRAPEFINGER
SOME OF THIS STUFF MAY NOT EVEN WIND UP IN THIS STORY-- BUT SO WHAT?
BY NOW, YOU'VE PROBABLY ALREADY PAID FOR THIS BOOK! HAHAHAHAHAHA-HAHAHA!
SCOTT SHAW!
PRUNEY PUNCH
WRITTEN AND DRAWN BY
SCOTT "COLE SLAW" SHAW
COLORED BY LAURIE "LETTUCE" E. SMITH
LETTERED BY TOM "TOMATO" ORZECHOWSKI AND
JANICE "CROUTON" CHIANG
EDITED BY JIM "SALAD CROP" SALICRUP
NNOYING ORANGE AS "SECRET AGENT OO-ORANGE"
ARSHMALLOW AS "MMM-MMM"
IDGET APPLE AS "QUE"
PPLE AS "HARD-CORE"
PASSION FRUIT AS "FRUITY O' LOOMIS
PEAR AS "FRUITY CIDER"
GRAPEFRUIT AS "ODD BLOB"
AND NERVILLE AS "SECRET AGENT UH-OH NERIVLLE"
BASED ON CARTOON NETWORK'S "ANNOYING ORANGE" TV SHOW
CREATED BY TOM SHEPPARD AND DANE BOEDIGHEIMER
AND THE ANNOYING ORANGE CHARACTERS
CREATED BY SPENCER GROVE, DANE BOEDIGHEIMER, AND TOM SHEPPARD
OUNDTRACK AVAILABLE FOR DOWNLOAD FROM GREEN THUMB MUSIC
"ANNOYING ORANGE" CREATED BY DANE BOEDIGHEIMER

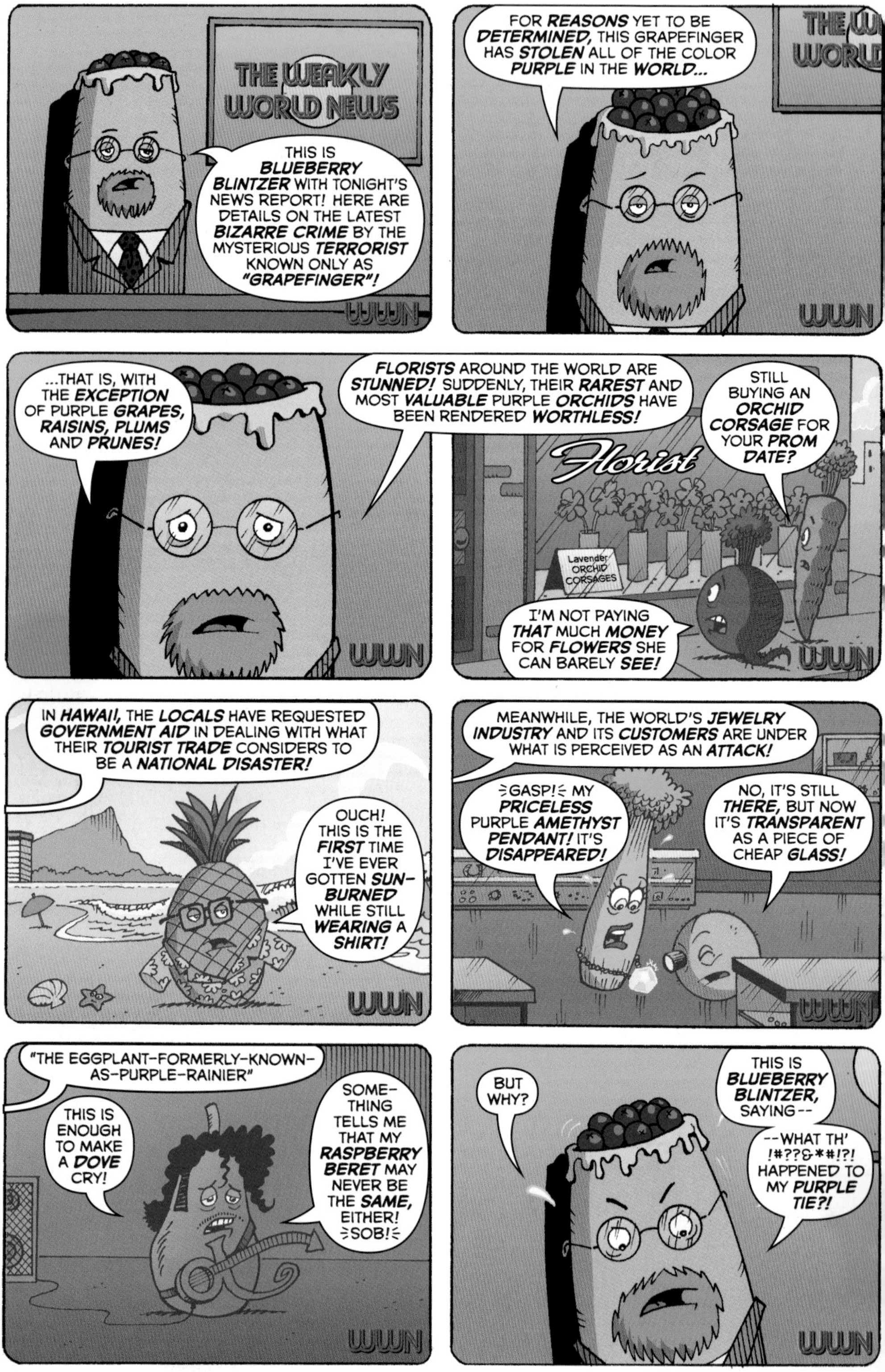
THE WEAKLY WORLD NEWS
THIS IS BLUEBERRY BLINTZER WITH TONIGHT'S NEWS REPORT! HERE ARE DETAILS ON THE LATEST BIZARRE CRIME BY THE MYSTERIOUS TERRORIST KNOWN ONLY AS "GRAPEFINGER"!
WWN
FOR REASONS YET TO BE DETERMINED, THIS GRAPEFINGER HAS STOLEN ALL OF THE COLOR PURPLE IN THE WORLD...
WWN
...THAT IS, WITH THE EXCEPTION OF PURPLE GRAPES, RAISINS, PLUMS AND PRUNES!
WWN
FLORISTS AROUND THE WORLD ARE STUNNED! SUDDENLY, THEIR RAREST AND MOST VALUABLE PURPLE ORCHIDS HAVE BEEN RENDERED WORTHLESS!
Florist
STILL BUYING AN ORCHID CORSAGE FOR YOUR PROM DATE?
Lavender ORCHID CORSAGES
I'M NOT PAYING THAT MUCH MONEY FOR FLOWERS SHE CAN BARELY SEE!
WWN
IN HAWAII, THE LOCALS HAVE REQUESTED GOVERNMENT AID IN DEALING WITH WHAT THEIR TOURIST TRADE CONSIDERS TO BE A NATIONAL DISASTER!
OUCH! THIS IS THE FIRST TIME I'VE EVER GOTTEN SUN-BURNED WHILE STILL WEARING A SHIRT!
WWN
MEANWHILE, THE WORLD'S JEWELRY INDUSTRY AND ITS CUSTOMERS ARE UNDER WHAT IS PERCEIVED AS AN ATTACK!
GASP! MY PRICELESS PURPLE AMETHYST PENDANT! IT'S DISAPPEARED!
NO, IT'S STILL THERE, BUT NOW IT'S TRANSPARENT AS A PIECE OF CHEAP GLASS!
WWN
"THE EGGPLANT-FORMERLY-KNOWN-AS-PURPLE-RAINIER"
THIS IS ENOUGH TO MAKE A DOVE CRY!
SOME-THING TELLS ME THAT MY RASPBERRY BERET MAY NEVER BE THE SAME, EITHER! SOB!
WWN
BUT WHY?
THIS IS BLUEBERRY BLINTZER, SAYING--
--WHAT TH' !#??&*#!?! HAPPENED TO MY PURPLE TIE?!
WWN

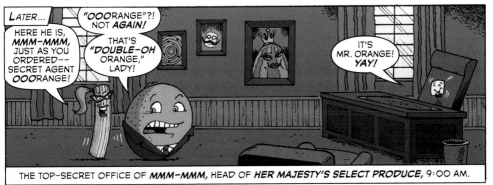

LATER...

HERE HE IS, *MMM-MMM*, JUST AS YOU ORDERED-- SECRET AGENT *OOORANGE!*

"OOORANGE"?! NOT *AGAIN!*

THAT'S *"DOUBLE-OH* ORANGE," LADY!

IT'S MR. ORANGE! *YAY!*

THE TOP-SECRET OFFICE OF *MMM-MMM,* HEAD OF *HER MAJESTY'S SELECT PRODUCE,* 9:00 AM.

DO YOU REMEMBER MY *PRIVATE SECRETARY, MISS MONEY-PENNE,* AGENT OO-ORANGE?

ONLY A *PRIVATE,* EH? DON'T WORRY, I WON'T *PULL RANK* ON YOU! HAHAHAHAHAHAHA!

JUST DON'T PULL ANY OF YOUR *SHENANIGANS* ON ME--

--YOU INEXPLICABLY CHARMING CITRUS FRUIT!

I'D LIKE TO OFFER MY *APOLOGIES* REGARDING THE *DISAPPEARANCE* OF *AGENT UH-OH-NERVILLE,* YOUR FORMER PARTNER. LIFE CAN BE A *BLEAK PIT OF DESPAIR,* EH, WOT?

"FORMER PARTNER"!?

SHOULD I CALL *SECURITY,* BOSS?

THAT KID'S *STILL* MY NUTTY *SPY BIZ* PARTNER AND I'LL DO *ANYTHING* TO *HELP* HIM!

CALM *DOWN,* AGENT OO-ORANGE! YOU'RE GETTING *AGITATED!*

OF *COURSE* I'M AGITATED! I'VE GOT A MINIATURIZED *WASHING MACHINE* IN MY *POCKET!* HAHAHAHAHAHAHA!

BUT I *INSIST* ON *VOLUNTEERING* TO PERSONALLY *SEARCH* FOR MOMMA NERVILLE'S LITTLE *BOY!*

NO, *YOUR* HIGH-PRIORITY MISSION IS TO LOOK INTO A NEW AND DANGEROUS *THREAT* TO FRUIT-KIND, A MYSTERIOUS *"PURPLE-THEFT"* MASTERMIND KNOWN ONLY AS *"GRAPEFINGER"!*

THE ENTIRE WORLD MIGHT BE *DOOMED!* YAY!

I'VE HEARD OF *"CHICKEN FINGERS,"* BUT *"GRAPE*FINGER"? NAW.

WHY IS HE *CALLED* "GRAPEFINGER," ANYWAY? GRAPES DON'T EVEN *HAVE* FINGERS!

DON'T LOOK NOW, BUT *WE* DON'T EVEN HAVE *HANDS!* HAHAHAHAHAHAHA!

BUT WHO *CARES?* EVER SEE ANYONE WITH HANDS DO-- *THIS?*

NUH-NUH- NUH-NUH- NUH...

OH, *MY!* THAT *IS* ODDLY SMASHING!

NUH-NUH-NUH-NUH-NUH...

PUH-LEASE, NOT *NOW*, AGENT OO-ORANGE! I'VE GOT CRUCIAL *EXPOSITION* TO DELIVER!

THIS IS *MELVIN GRAPEFINGER*, AN *ECCENTRIC ZILLIONAIRE SOFT DRINK MANUFACTURER!* HE ALSO HAS A *PENCHANT* FOR *SURROUNDING* HIMSELF WITH THE COLOR *PURPLE! THAT'S* WHY WE THINK HE'S *INVOLVED* IN THESE SO-CALLED *"PURPLE-THEFTS"!*

OOOH, HE'S ONE OF *THOSE* PEOPLE? PEOPLE WHO NEED *PURPLE?* THEY'RE THE *LUCKIEST* PEOPLE IN THE *WORLD!* HAHAHAHAHAHAHA!

AND THIS IS *FEZZIWIG*, MR. GRAPEFINGER'S PEDIGREED *PET!*

SILLY-LOOKING LI'L *BUGGER*, AIN'T HE? HAHAHAHA-HAHAHA!

QUITE THE *OPPOSITE*, MR. ORANGE. THAT RAVENOUS *WORM* COULD *STRIP* A FRUIT TO ITS *SEEDS* IN MERE *SECONDS!*

⋛ULP!⋚

EXACTLY. *YAY!*

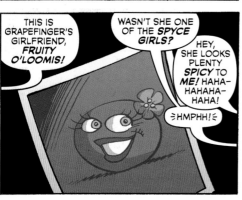

THIS IS GRAPEFINGER'S GIRLFRIEND, *FRUITY O'LOOMIS!*

WASN'T SHE ONE OF THE *SPYCE GIRLS?*

HEY, SHE LOOKS PLENTY *SPICY* TO *ME!* HAHA-HAHAHA-HAHA!

⋛HMPHH!⋚

AND THIS IS GRAPEFINGER'S *BODYGUARD!* THE BULBOUS *BRUTE'S* NAME IS *ODDBLOB!*

NICE *HAT*-- I'VE SEEN BETTER *BOWLERS* IN *BOWLING* ALLEYS! AND THAT GOES FOR *BIG, ROUND THINGS* WITH THREE *HOLES* IN 'EM, TOO! HAHAHAHAHAHA!

DURING YOUR INVESTIGATION, SPECIAL AGENT *MELONY HARVEST* WILL BE YOUR *CONTACT* IN THE FIELD!

I BET SHE'D BE *OUTSTANDING* IN *ANY* FIELD! HAHAHAHAHA-HAHA!

LIKE A *SCARECROW?*

YOU'RE NOT *JEALOUS*, ARE YOU, MISS MONEY-PENNE? AFTER ALL, YOU'RE DEFINITELY NOT *PASTA* YOUR *PRIME!*

AGAIN, ⋛HMPHH!⋚

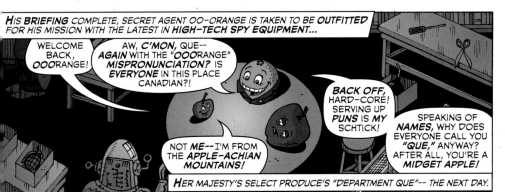

HIS BRIEFING COMPLETE, SECRET AGENT OO-ORANGE IS TAKEN TO BE OUTFITTED FOR HIS MISSION WITH THE LATEST IN HIGH-TECH SPY EQUIPMENT...
WELCOME BACK, OOORANGE!
AW, C'MON, QUE-- AGAIN WITH THE "OOORANGE" MISPRONUNCIATION? IS EVERYONE IN THIS PLACE CANADIAN?!
NOT ME--I'M FROM THE APPLE-ACHIAN MOUNTAINS!
BACK OFF, HARD-CORE! SERVING UP PUNS IS MY SCHTICK!
SPEAKING OF NAMES, WHY DOES EVERYONE CALL YOU "QUE," ANYWAY? AFTER ALL, YOU'RE A MIDGET APPLE!
HER MAJESTY'S SELECT PRODUCE'S "DEPARTMENT QUE"-- THE NEXT DAY.
BACK WHEN I APPLIED FOR THIS JOB, I LISTED MYSELF AS A QUANDONG!
WHAT?
OH, IT'S A TYPE OF DESERT PEACH... I THOUGHT IT MIGHT MAKE ME SEEM EXOTIC! THE CHICKS REALLY DIG IT!
IT'S A PEACH OF A NAME! HAHAHAHAHA-HAHA!
NEXT...
THIS PERSONAL MINI-COPTER IS POWERFUL ENOUGH TO LIFT YOU TEN STORIES HIGH!
I'D BE A HIGH SPY!
I'M GETTING AIR-SICK, QUE! HAVE YOU INVENTED A HIGH-TECH BARF BAG YET?
NEXT...
UPON MASTICATION, THIS CHEWING GUM TURNS INTO A PLASTIC EXPLOSIVE!
KA-BOOOM
SOUNDS LIKE A BLAST TO ME!
HAH HAHAH HAHA!
AT LEAST THIS JOB INCLUDES DENTAL BENEFITS! GROAN!
NEXT...
ALTHOUGH IT APPEARS TO BE AN ORDINARY BANANA, THIS IS ACTUALLY A HIGH-POWER HAND GUN!
YEOW!
I'D LIKE TO MONKEY AROUND WITH THAT!
HAH HAHAH HAHA!
JUST DON'T SLIP ON THE PEEL!
WHOAAAH!
SLIP
NEXT...
THIS ARTIFICIAL TOOTH CONTAINS A TWO-WAY RADIO FOR COVERT COMMUNICATION!
I FOUND MY THRILL...ON BLUEBERRY HILL...
LET'S HOPE THE TOOTH FAIRY APPROVES!
MAKE IT STOP!
NEXT...
NOW THIS IS A REAL BREAK-THROUGH-- THE WORLD'S FIRST MAGNETIC UNDER-WEAR!
ARE WE DONE YET?
NOW IF WE ONLY HAD A USE FOR 'EM!
YEAH, I'VE ALREADY GOT A MAGNETIC PERSONALITY! HAHAHAHAHAHAHA!!

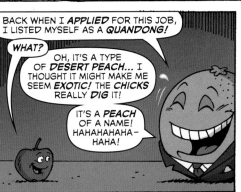

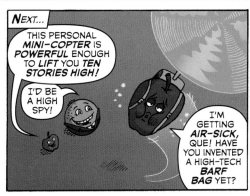

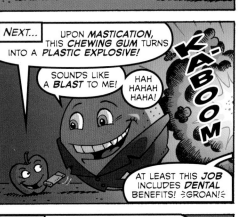

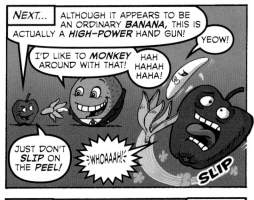

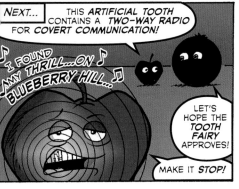

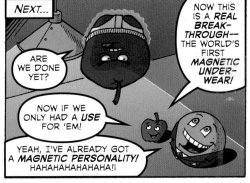

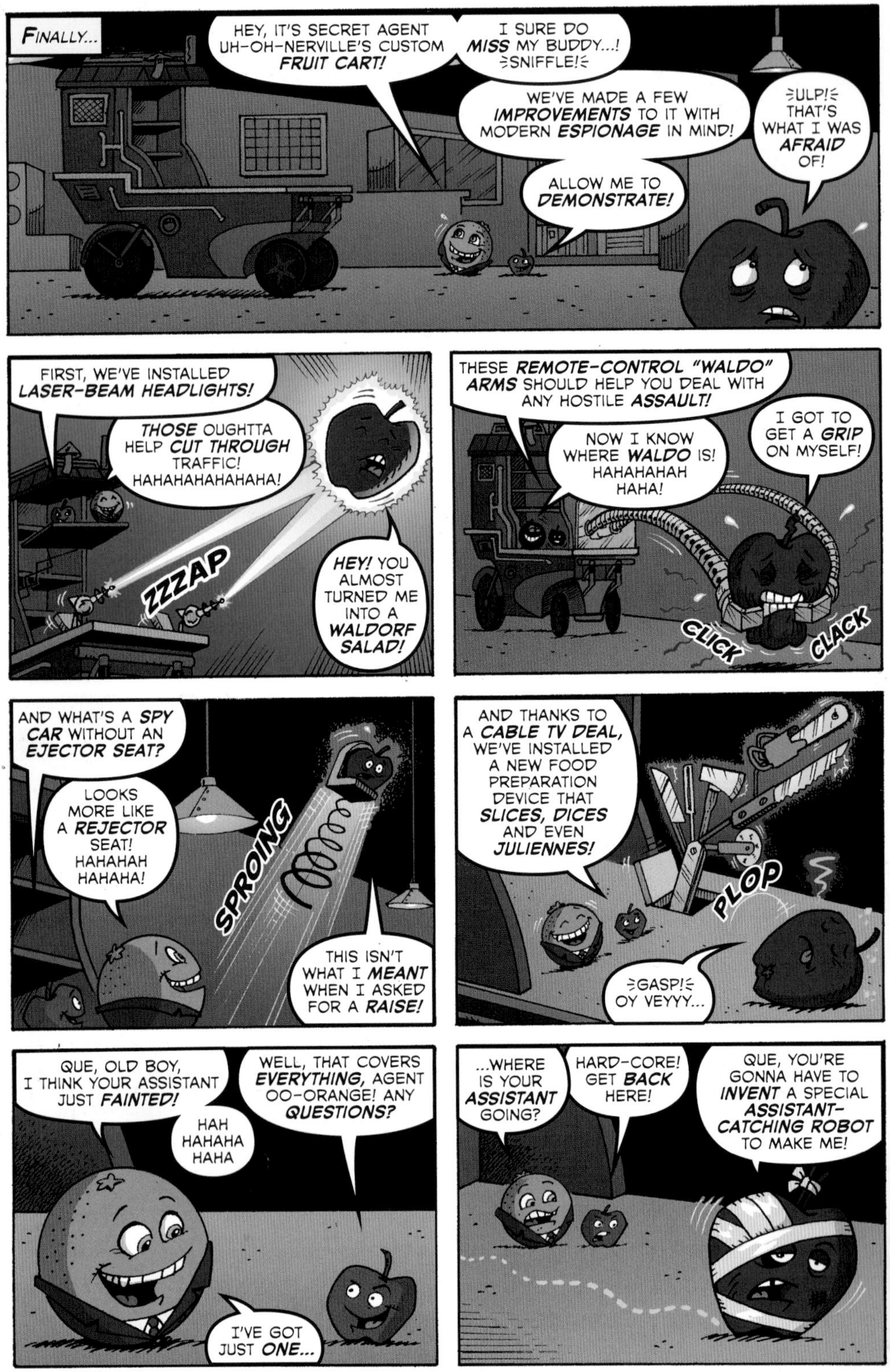
FINALLY...
HEY, IT'S SECRET AGENT UH-OH-NERVILLE'S CUSTOM FRUIT CART!
I SURE DO MISS MY BUDDY...! ≥SNIFFLE!≤
WE'VE MADE A FEW IMPROVEMENTS TO IT WITH MODERN ESPIONAGE IN MIND!
ALLOW ME TO DEMONSTRATE!
≥ULP!≤ THAT'S WHAT I WAS AFRAID OF!
FIRST, WE'VE INSTALLED LASER-BEAM HEADLIGHTS!
THOSE OUGHTTA HELP CUT THROUGH TRAFFIC! HAHAHAHAHAHAHA!
ZZZAP
HEY! YOU ALMOST TURNED ME INTO A WALDORF SALAD!
THESE REMOTE-CONTROL "WALDO" ARMS SHOULD HELP YOU DEAL WITH ANY HOSTILE ASSAULT!
NOW I KNOW WHERE WALDO IS! HAHAHAHAH HAHA!
I GOT TO GET A GRIP ON MYSELF!
CLICK
CLACK
AND WHAT'S A SPY CAR WITHOUT AN EJECTOR SEAT?
LOOKS MORE LIKE A REJECTOR SEAT! HAHAHAH HAHAHA!
SPROING
THIS ISN'T WHAT I MEANT WHEN I ASKED FOR A RAISE!
AND THANKS TO A CABLE TV DEAL, WE'VE INSTALLED A NEW FOOD PREPARATION DEVICE THAT SLICES, DICES AND EVEN JULIENNES!
PLOP
≥GASP!≤ OY VEYYY...
QUE, OLD BOY, I THINK YOUR ASSISTANT JUST FAINTED!
HAH HAHAHA HAHA
WELL, THAT COVERS EVERYTHING, AGENT OO-ORANGE! ANY QUESTIONS?
I'VE GOT JUST ONE...
...WHERE IS YOUR ASSISTANT GOING?
HARD-CORE! GET BACK HERE!
QUE, YOU'RE GONNA HAVE TO INVENT A SPECIAL ASSISTANT-CATCHING ROBOT TO MAKE ME!

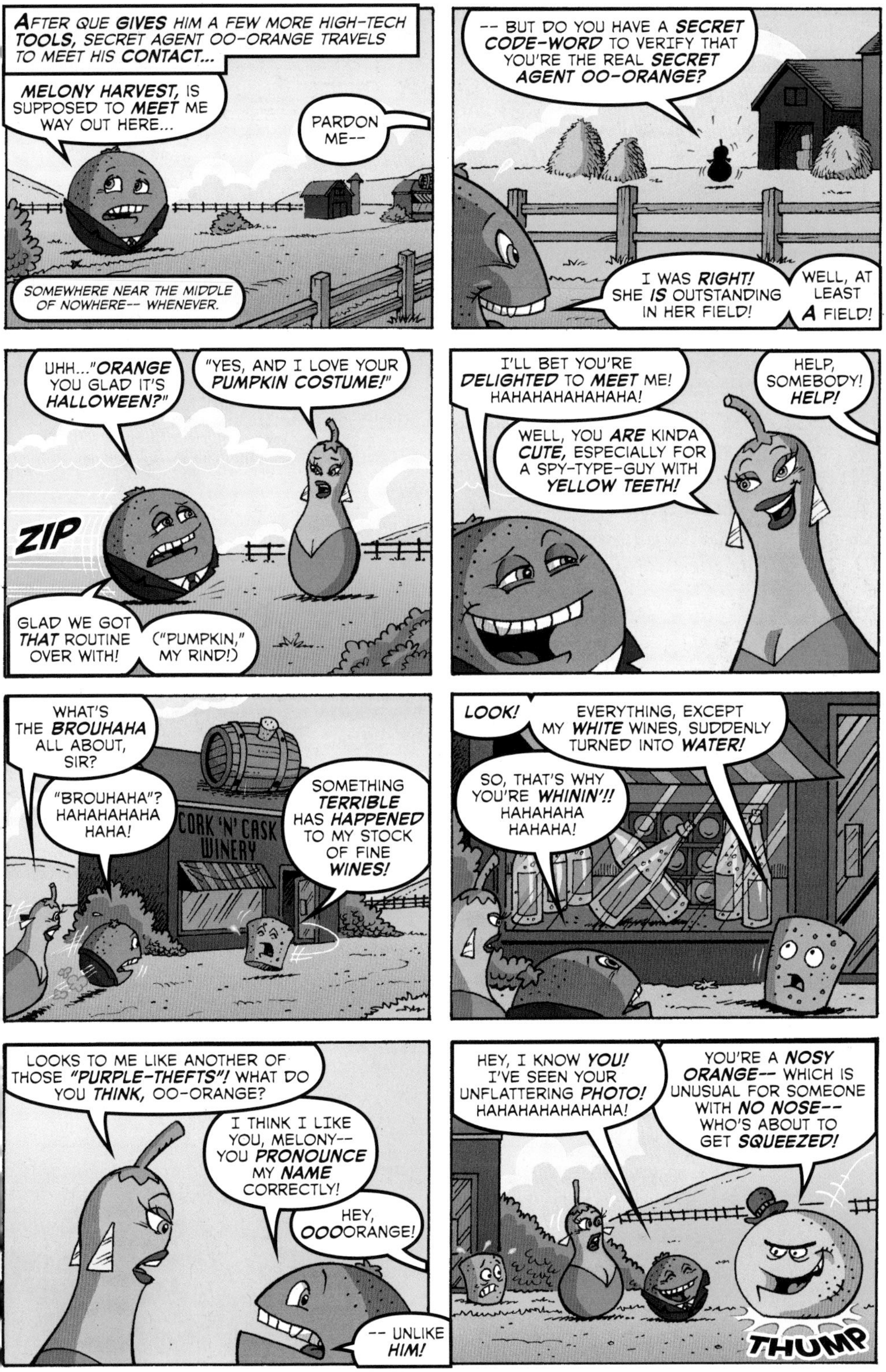

AFTER QUE GIVES HIM A FEW MORE HIGH-TECH TOOLS, SECRET AGENT OO-ORANGE TRAVELS TO MEET HIS CONTACT...
MELONY HARVEST, IS SUPPOSED TO MEET ME WAY OUT HERE...
PARDON ME--
SOMEWHERE NEAR THE MIDDLE OF NOWHERE-- WHENEVER.
-- BUT DO YOU HAVE A SECRET CODE-WORD TO VERIFY THAT YOU'RE THE REAL SECRET AGENT OO-ORANGE?
I WAS RIGHT! SHE IS OUTSTANDING IN HER FIELD!
WELL, AT LEAST A FIELD!
UHH..."ORANGE YOU GLAD IT'S HALLOWEEN?"
"YES, AND I LOVE YOUR PUMPKIN COSTUME!"
ZIP
GLAD WE GOT THAT ROUTINE OVER WITH!
("PUMPKIN," MY RIND!)
I'LL BET YOU'RE DELIGHTED TO MEET ME! HAHAHAHAHAHAHA!
HELP, SOMEBODY! HELP!
WELL, YOU ARE KINDA CUTE, ESPECIALLY FOR A SPY-TYPE-GUY WITH YELLOW TEETH!
WHAT'S THE BROUHAHA ALL ABOUT, SIR?
"BROUHAHA"? HAHAHAHAHA HAHA!
SOMETHING TERRIBLE HAS HAPPENED TO MY STOCK OF FINE WINES!
CORK 'N' CASK WINERY
LOOK!
EVERYTHING, EXCEPT MY WHITE WINES, SUDDENLY TURNED INTO WATER!
SO, THAT'S WHY YOU'RE WHININ'!! HAHAHAHA HAHAHA!
LOOKS TO ME LIKE ANOTHER OF THOSE "PURPLE-THEFTS"! WHAT DO YOU THINK, OO-ORANGE?
I THINK I LIKE YOU, MELONY-- YOU PRONOUNCE MY NAME CORRECTLY!
HEY, OOOORANGE!
-- UNLIKE HIM!
HEY, I KNOW YOU! I'VE SEEN YOUR UNFLATTERING PHOTO! HAHAHAHAHAHAHA!
YOU'RE A NOSY ORANGE-- WHICH IS UNUSUAL FOR SOMEONE WITH NO NOSE-- WHO'S ABOUT TO GET SQUEEZED!
THUMP

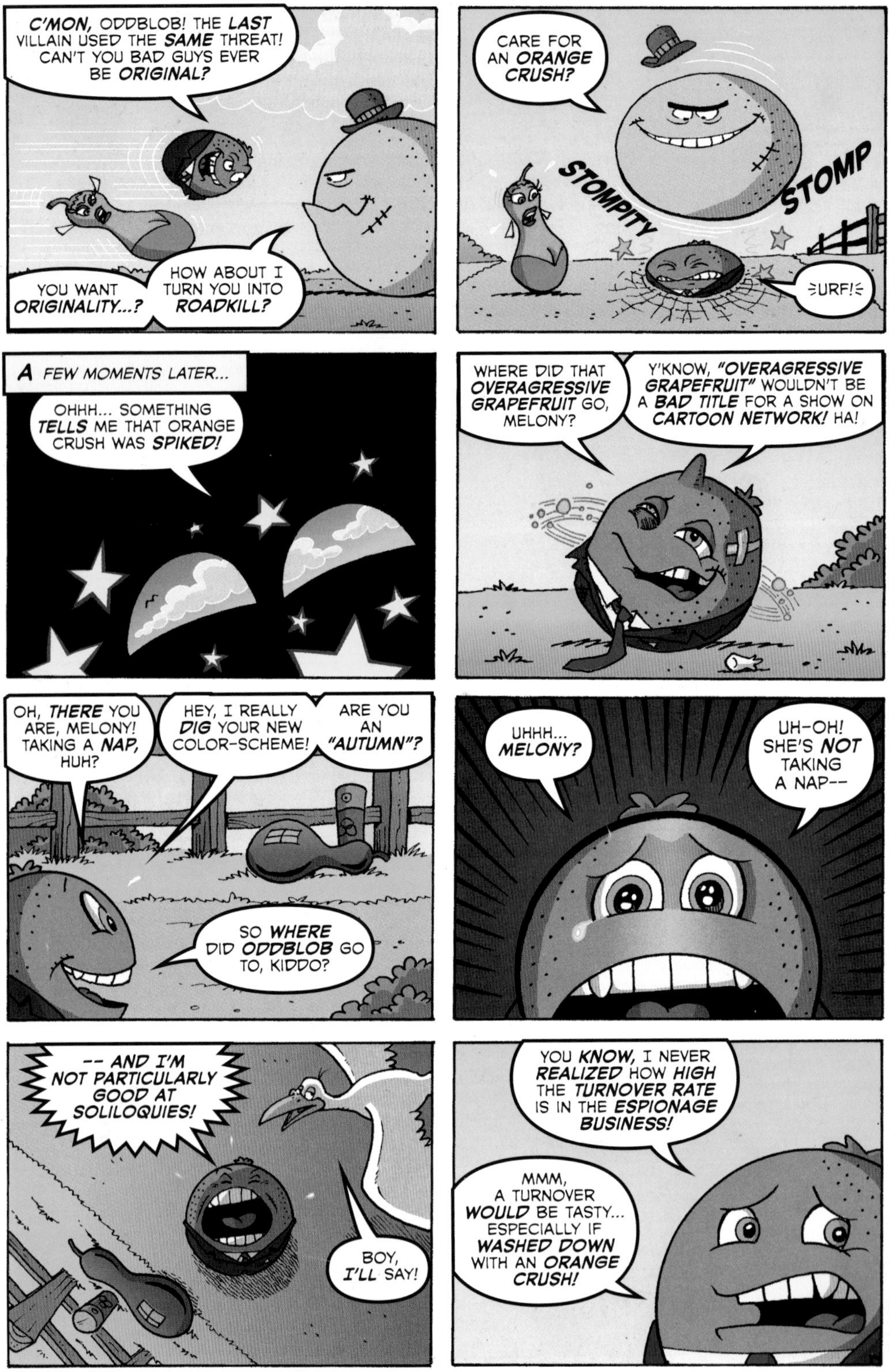
C'MON, ODDBLOB! THE LAST VILLAIN USED THE SAME THREAT! CAN'T YOU BAD GUYS EVER BE ORIGINAL?
YOU WANT ORIGINALITY...?
HOW ABOUT I TURN YOU INTO ROADKILL?
CARE FOR AN ORANGE CRUSH?
STOMPITY
STOMP
URF!
A FEW MOMENTS LATER...
OHHH... SOMETHING TELLS ME THAT ORANGE CRUSH WAS SPIKED!
WHERE DID THAT OVERAGRESSIVE GRAPEFRUIT GO, MELONY?
Y'KNOW, "OVERAGRESSIVE GRAPEFRUIT" WOULDN'T BE A BAD TITLE FOR A SHOW ON CARTOON NETWORK! HA!
OH, THERE YOU ARE, MELONY! TAKING A NAP, HUH?
HEY, I REALLY DIG YOUR NEW COLOR-SCHEME!
ARE YOU AN "AUTUMN"?
SO WHERE DID ODDBLOB GO TO, KIDDO?
UHHH... MELONY?
UH-OH! SHE'S NOT TAKING A NAP--
-- AND I'M NOT PARTICULARLY GOOD AT SOLILOQUIES!
BOY, I'LL SAY!
YOU KNOW, I NEVER REALIZED HOW HIGH THE TURNOVER RATE IS IN THE ESPIONAGE BUSINESS!
MMM, A TURNOVER WOULD BE TASTY... ESPECIALLY IF WASHED DOWN WITH AN ORANGE CRUSH!

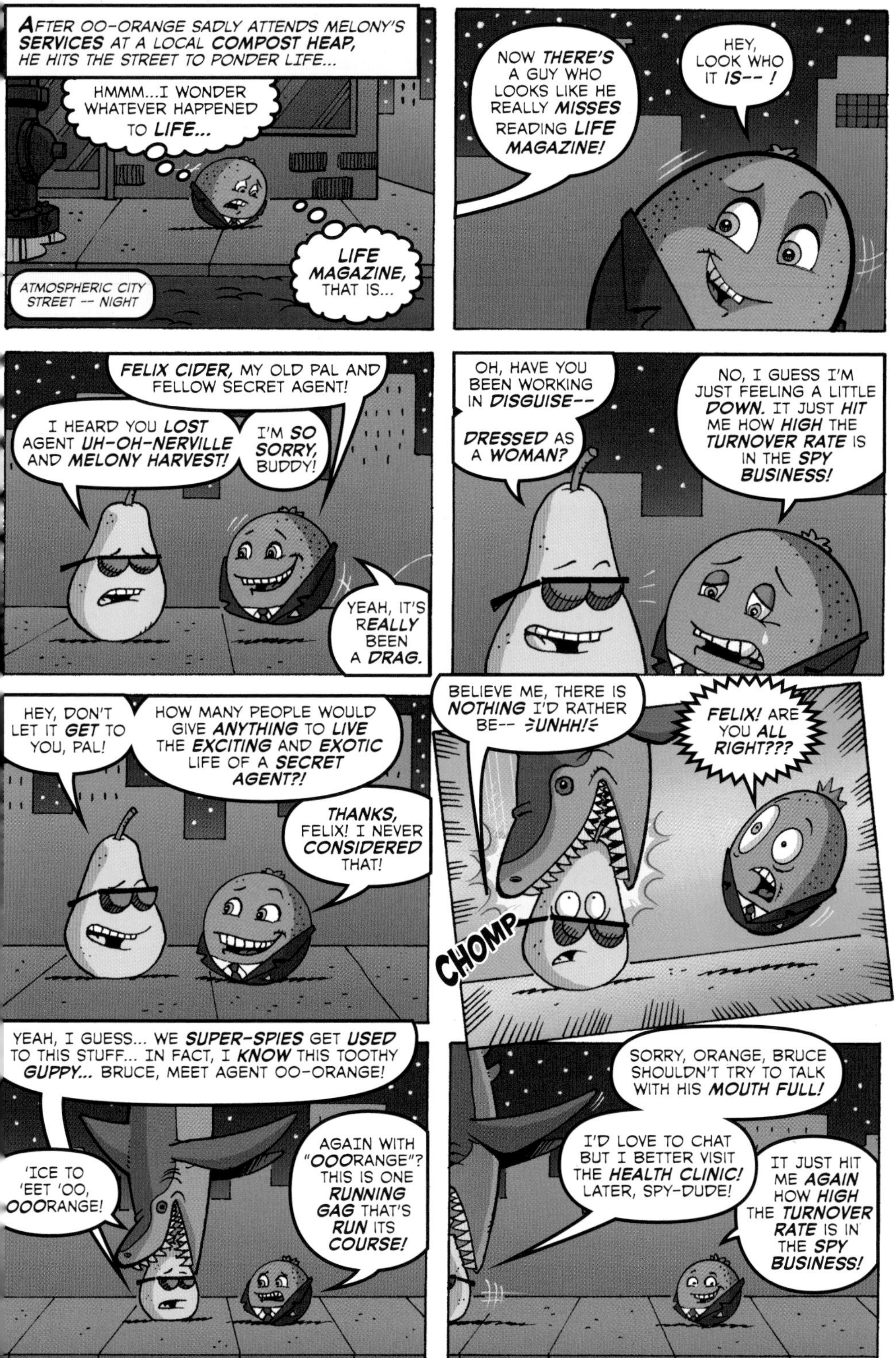
AFTER OO-ORANGE SADLY ATTENDS MELONY'S SERVICES AT A LOCAL COMPOST HEAP, HE HITS THE STREET TO PONDER LIFE...
HMMM...I WONDER WHATEVER HAPPENED TO LIFE...
LIFE MAGAZINE, THAT IS...
ATMOSPHERIC CITY STREET -- NIGHT
HEY, LOOK WHO IT IS-- !
NOW THERE'S A GUY WHO LOOKS LIKE HE REALLY MISSES READING LIFE MAGAZINE!
FELIX CIDER, MY OLD PAL AND FELLOW SECRET AGENT!
I HEARD YOU LOST AGENT UH-OH-NERVILLE AND MELONY HARVEST!
I'M SO SORRY, BUDDY!
YEAH, IT'S REALLY BEEN A DRAG.
OH, HAVE YOU BEEN WORKING IN DISGUISE--
DRESSED AS A WOMAN?
NO, I GUESS I'M JUST FEELING A LITTLE DOWN. IT JUST HIT ME HOW HIGH THE TURNOVER RATE IS IN THE SPY BUSINESS!
HEY, DON'T LET IT GET TO YOU, PAL!
HOW MANY PEOPLE WOULD GIVE ANYTHING TO LIVE THE EXCITING AND EXOTIC LIFE OF A SECRET AGENT?!
THANKS, FELIX! I NEVER CONSIDERED THAT!
BELIEVE ME, THERE IS NOTHING I'D RATHER BE-- UNHH!
FELIX! ARE YOU ALL RIGHT???
CHOMP
YEAH, I GUESS... WE SUPER-SPIES GET USED TO THIS STUFF... IN FACT, I KNOW THIS TOOTHY GUPPY... BRUCE, MEET AGENT OO-ORANGE!
'ICE TO 'EET 'OO, OOORANGE!
AGAIN WITH "OOORANGE"? THIS IS ONE RUNNING GAG THAT'S RUN ITS COURSE!
SORRY, ORANGE, BRUCE SHOULDN'T TRY TO TALK WITH HIS MOUTH FULL!
I'D LOVE TO CHAT BUT I BETTER VISIT THE HEALTH CLINIC! LATER, SPY-DUDE!
IT JUST HIT ME AGAIN HOW HIGH THE TURNOVER RATE IS IN THE SPY BUSINESS!

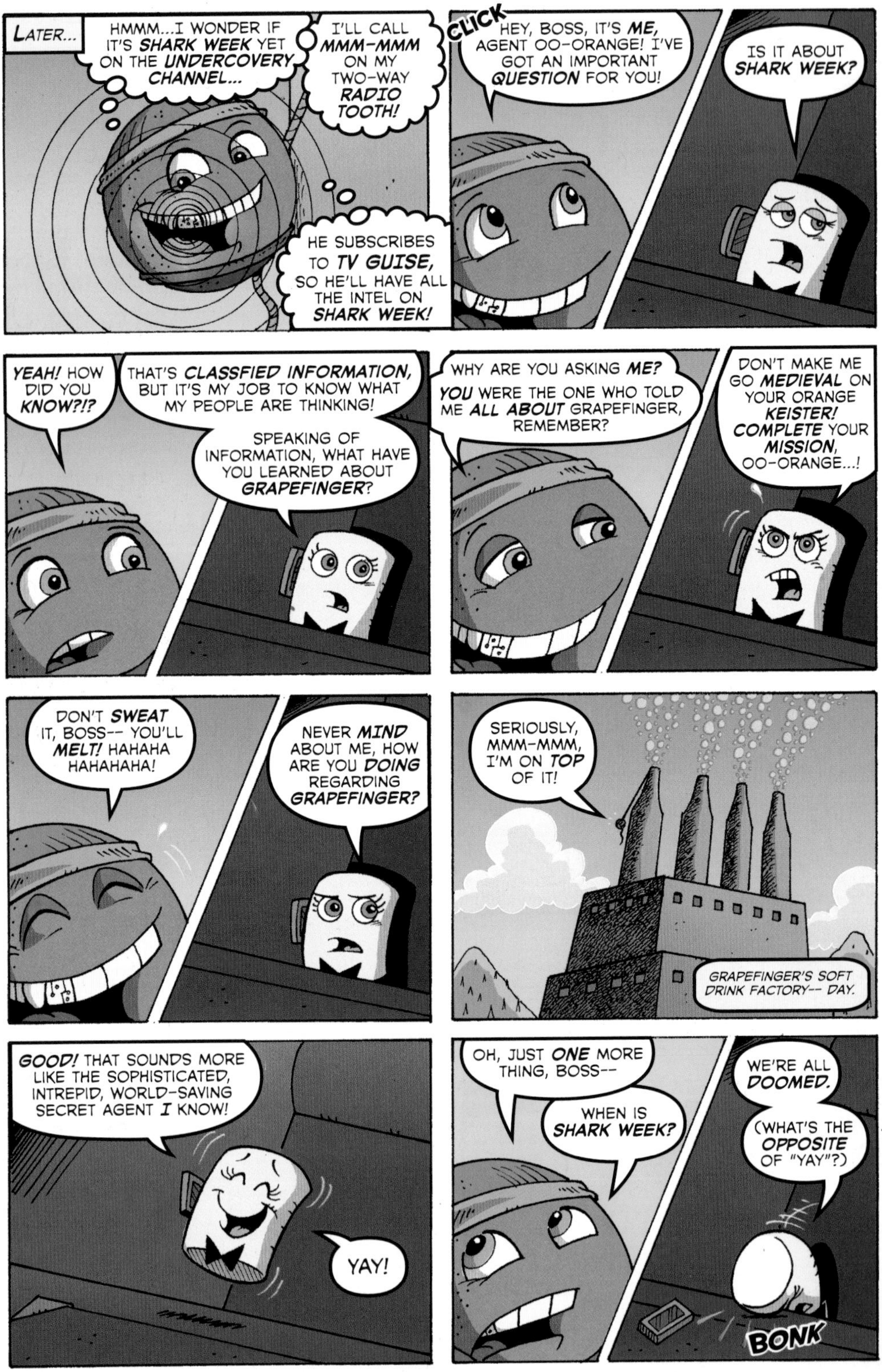
LATER...
HMMM...I WONDER IF IT'S SHARK WEEK YET ON THE UNDERCOVERY CHANNEL...
I'LL CALL MMM-MMM ON MY TWO-WAY RADIO TOOTH!
HE SUBSCRIBES TO TV GUISE, SO HE'LL HAVE ALL THE INTEL ON SHARK WEEK!
CLICK
HEY, BOSS, IT'S ME, AGENT OO-ORANGE! I'VE GOT AN IMPORTANT QUESTION FOR YOU!
IS IT ABOUT SHARK WEEK?
YEAH! HOW DID YOU KNOW?!?
THAT'S CLASSFIED INFORMATION, BUT IT'S MY JOB TO KNOW WHAT MY PEOPLE ARE THINKING!
SPEAKING OF INFORMATION, WHAT HAVE YOU LEARNED ABOUT GRAPEFINGER?
WHY ARE YOU ASKING ME?
YOU WERE THE ONE WHO TOLD ME ALL ABOUT GRAPEFINGER, REMEMBER?
DON'T MAKE ME GO MEDIEVAL ON YOUR ORANGE KEISTER! COMPLETE YOUR MISSION, OO-ORANGE...!
DON'T SWEAT IT, BOSS-- YOU'LL MELT! HAHAHA HAHAHAHA!
NEVER MIND ABOUT ME, HOW ARE YOU DOING REGARDING GRAPEFINGER?
SERIOUSLY, MMM-MMM, I'M ON TOP OF IT!
GRAPEFINGER'S SOFT DRINK FACTORY-- DAY.
GOOD! THAT SOUNDS MORE LIKE THE SOPHISTICATED, INTREPID, WORLD-SAVING SECRET AGENT I KNOW!
YAY!
OH, JUST ONE MORE THING, BOSS--
WHEN IS SHARK WEEK?
WE'RE ALL DOOMED.
(WHAT'S THE OPPOSITE OF "YAY"?)
BONK

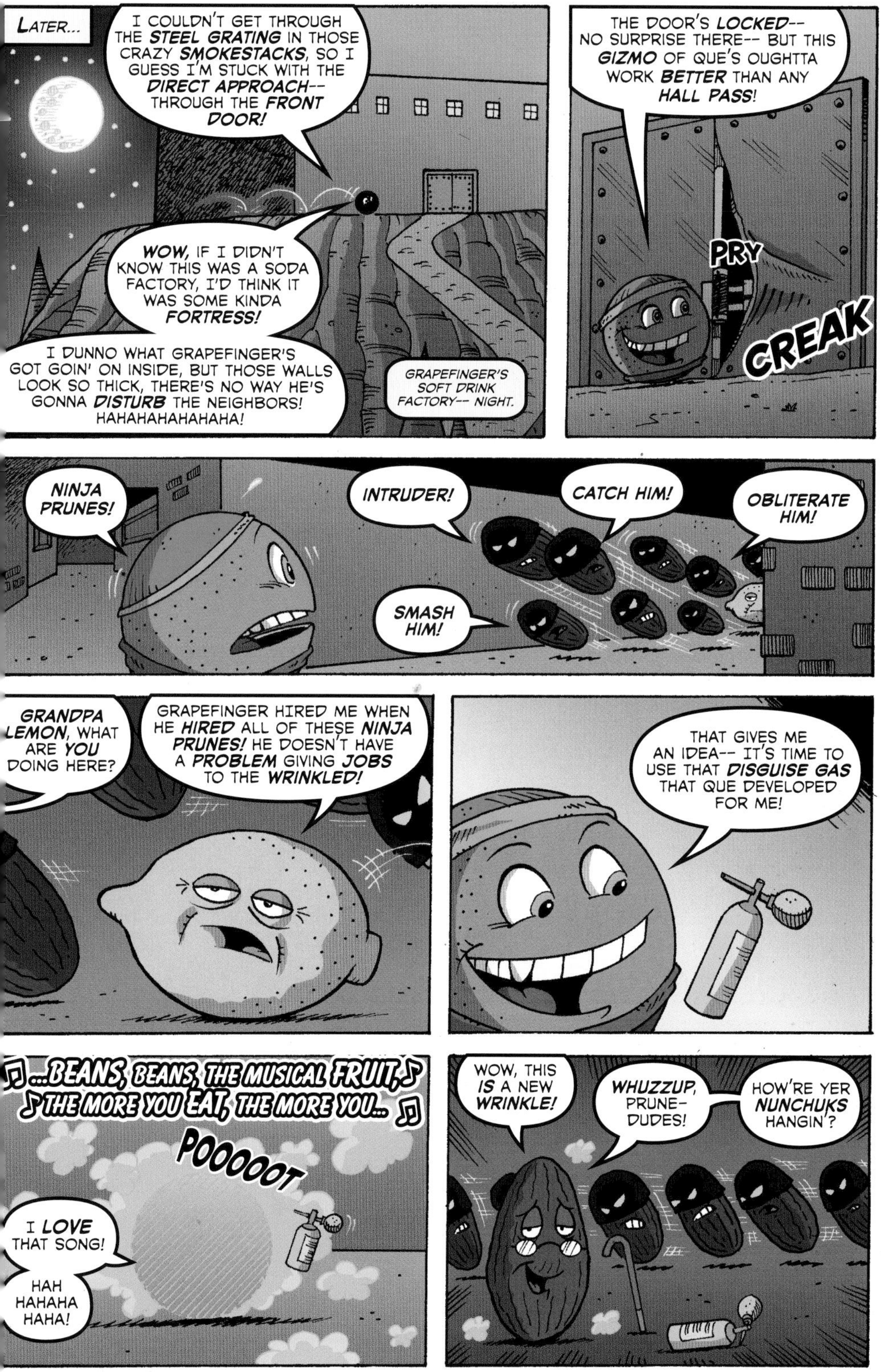
LATER...
I COULDN'T GET THROUGH THE STEEL GRATING IN THOSE CRAZY SMOKESTACKS, SO I GUESS I'M STUCK WITH THE DIRECT APPROACH-- THROUGH THE FRONT DOOR!
WOW, IF I DIDN'T KNOW THIS WAS A SODA FACTORY, I'D THINK IT WAS SOME KINDA FORTRESS!
I DUNNO WHAT GRAPEFINGER'S GOT GOIN' ON INSIDE, BUT THOSE WALLS LOOK SO THICK, THERE'S NO WAY HE'S GONNA DISTURB THE NEIGHBORS! HAHAHAHAHAHAHA!
GRAPEFINGER'S SOFT DRINK FACTORY-- NIGHT.
THE DOOR'S LOCKED-- NO SURPRISE THERE-- BUT THIS GIZMO OF QUE'S OUGHTTA WORK BETTER THAN ANY HALL PASS!
PRY
CREAK
NINJA PRUNES!
INTRUDER!
CATCH HIM!
OBLITERATE HIM!
SMASH HIM!
GRANDPA LEMON, WHAT ARE YOU DOING HERE?
GRAPEFINGER HIRED ME WHEN HE HIRED ALL OF THESE NINJA PRUNES! HE DOESN'T HAVE A PROBLEM GIVING JOBS TO THE WRINKLED!
THAT GIVES ME AN IDEA-- IT'S TIME TO USE THAT DISGUISE GAS THAT QUE DEVELOPED FOR ME!
♫ ...BEANS, BEANS, THE MUSICAL FRUIT, ♪
♪ THE MORE YOU EAT, THE MORE YOU... ♫
POOOOOT
I LOVE THAT SONG!
HAH HAHAHA HAHA!
WOW, THIS IS A NEW WRINKLE!
WHUZZUP, PRUNE-DUDES!
HOW'RE YER NUNCHUKS HANGIN'?

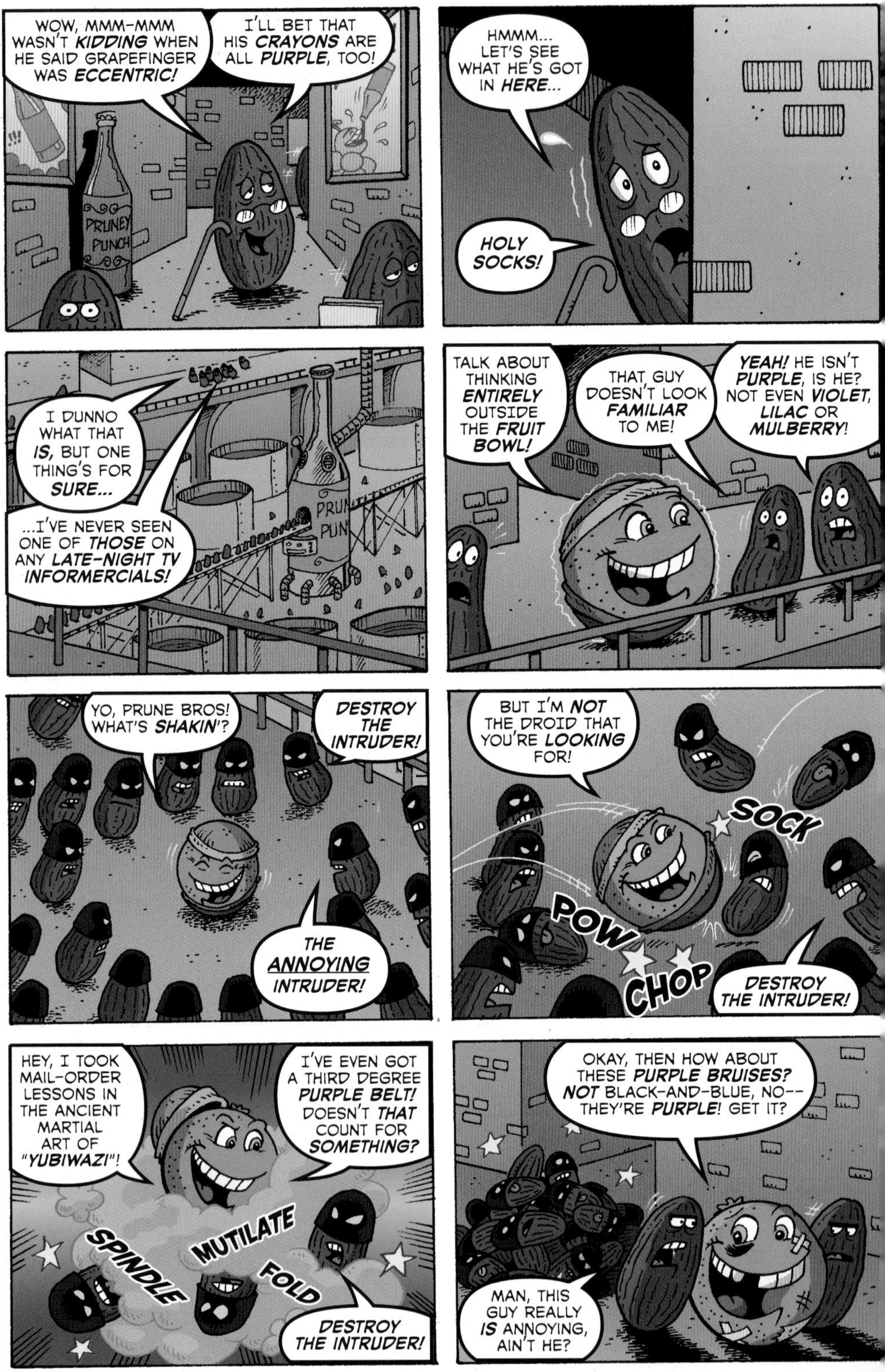
WOW, MMM-MMM WASN'T KIDDING WHEN HE SAID GRAPEFINGER WAS ECCENTRIC!
I'LL BET THAT HIS CRAYONS ARE ALL PURPLE, TOO!
PRUNEY PUNCH
HMMM... LET'S SEE WHAT HE'S GOT IN HERE...
HOLY SOCKS!
I DUNNO WHAT THAT IS, BUT ONE THING'S FOR SURE...
...I'VE NEVER SEEN ONE OF THOSE ON ANY LATE-NIGHT TV INFORMERCIALS!
TALK ABOUT THINKING ENTIRELY OUTSIDE THE FRUIT BOWL!
THAT GUY DOESN'T LOOK FAMILIAR TO ME!
YEAH! HE ISN'T PURPLE, IS HE? NOT EVEN VIOLET, LILAC OR MULBERRY!
YO, PRUNE BROS! WHAT'S SHAKIN'?
DESTROY THE INTRUDER!
THE ANNOYING INTRUDER!
BUT I'M NOT THE DROID THAT YOU'RE LOOKING FOR!
SOCK
POW
CHOP
DESTROY THE INTRUDER!
HEY, I TOOK MAIL-ORDER LESSONS IN THE ANCIENT MARTIAL ART OF "YUBIWAZI"!
I'VE EVEN GOT A THIRD DEGREE PURPLE BELT! DOESN'T THAT COUNT FOR SOMETHING?
SPINDLE
MUTILATE
FOLD
DESTROY THE INTRUDER!
OKAY, THEN HOW ABOUT THESE PURPLE BRUISES? NOT BLACK-AND-BLUE, NO-- THEY'RE PURPLE! GET IT?
MAN, THIS GUY REALLY IS ANNOYING, AIN'T HE?

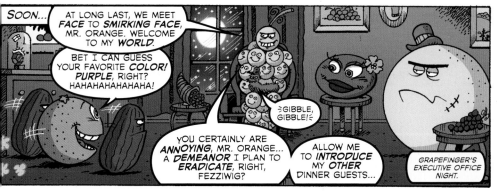

SOON...

AT LONG LAST, WE MEET *FACE* TO *SMIRKING FACE*, MR. ORANGE. WELCOME TO MY *WORLD*.

BET I CAN GUESS YOUR FAVORITE *COLOR!* *PURPLE*, RIGHT? HAHAHAHAHAHAHA!

⋛GIBBLE, GIBBLE!⋚

YOU CERTAINLY ARE *ANNOYING*, MR. ORANGE... A *DEMEANOR* I PLAN TO *ERADICATE*, RIGHT, FEZZIWIG?

ALLOW ME TO *INTRODUCE* MY *OTHER* DINNER GUESTS...

GRAPEFINGER'S EXECUTIVE OFFICE NIGHT.

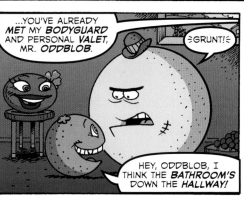

...YOU'VE ALREADY *MET* MY *BODYGUARD* AND PERSONAL *VALET*, MR. *ODDBLOB*.

⋛GRUNT!⋚

HEY, ODDBLOB, I THINK THE *BATHROOM'S* DOWN THE *HALLWAY!*

NEVER MIND HIM, *WHO'S* THE *HOT CHIQUITA?* (NOT THAT I'M SAYIN' SHE LOOKS LIKE A *BANANA!*)

C'MON, *GIVE!*

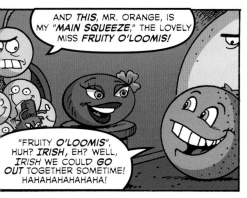

AND *THIS*, MR. ORANGE, IS MY *"MAIN SQUEEZE,"* THE LOVELY MISS *FRUITY O'LOOMIS!*

"FRUITY *O'LOOMIS*", HUH? *IRISH*, EH? WELL, *IRISH* WE COULD *GO OUT* TOGETHER SOMETIME! HAHAHAHAHAHAHA!

YOU'RE RATHER *FRESH*, AREN'T YOU, MR. ORANGE?

YOU *BET!* I'M ONE *FRESH FRUIT!* THE *FRESHEST*, EVEN! HEY, LEMME SHOW YOU A *TRICK*, FRUITY TOOT-TOOT!

NUH-NUH-NUH-NUH-NUH...

OOOH! THAT *IS* SURPRISINGLY *BRILLIANT!*

NUH-NUH-NUH-NUH-NUH...FEEL FREE TO *JOIN* ME, FRUITILICIOUS!... NUH-NUH-NUH-NUH-NUH...

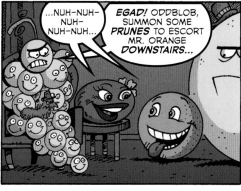

...NUH-NUH-NUH-NUH-NUH...

EGAD! ODDBLOB, SUMMON SOME *PRUNES* TO ESCORT MR. *ORANGE DOWNSTAIRS...*

HEY, I CAN'T *BLAME* GRAPEFINGER FOR TAKING HIS PRIVATE *ELEVATOR*... ONE *MISSTEP* AND THERE'D BE *GRAPE JUICE* ALL OVER THE *WALLS* (NOT THAT THEY'D LOOK MUCH *DIFFERENT!*)

HAH HAHAH HAHA!

FINALLY, DEEP UNDERGROUND...

SO, GRAPEFINGER, IS THIS *CRUMMY-LOOKING*, PLACE YOUR *BASEMENT*?

NO, MR. ORANGE, *THIS* IS WHAT I LIKE TO CALL...

...MY *"QUESTIONS-AND-ANSWERS ROOM"*!

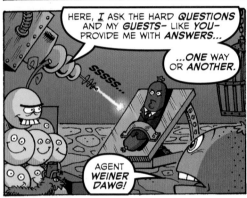

HERE, *I* ASK THE HARD *QUESTIONS* AND MY *GUESTS*– LIKE *YOU*– PROVIDE ME WITH *ANSWERS*...

...*ONE* WAY OR *ANOTHER*.

SSSSS...

AGENT *WEINER DAWG*!

SSSSS...

DO YOU EXPECT ME TO *TALK*?

NO, MR. *DAWG*, I EXPECT YOU TO *BUTTERFLY*!

SSSSS...

Y'KNOW, GRAPEFINGER, I'M REALLY *IMPRESSED* WITH YOUR OPERATION! I'D *LOVE* TO GET A PERSONAL *TOUR* BY THE *GENIUS* BEHIND IT!

OH, YOU *SAW* THAT, DID YOU?

HE'S *BUYING* IT! THAT OUGHTTA BUY ME SOME *TIME* TO FIGURE OUT WHAT'S *NEXT*!

HE'S *STALLING*! THAT WILL *BUY* ME SOME *TIME* TO FIGURE OUT WHAT HE *KNOWS*!

I'M STARTING TO THINK THAT IT'D BE *SMARTER* TO *PRETEND* TO *COOPERATE* WITH THIS *BIG BUNCH* OF *GRAPES* THAN TO *RESIST* HIM!

LESS *PAINFUL*, TOO!

I'D *ENJOY* THAT, MR. ORANGE. BUT *FIRST*, I INSIST YOU JOIN ME FOR *DINNER*!

"JOIN" YOU? *WHY*? HAVE YOU *COME APART*? BUT SURE, WHY *NOT*? LET'S HOPE YOU'RE SERVING SOME OF THAT FANCY *FRENCH FERTILIZER*!

HAH HAHAHA HAHA!

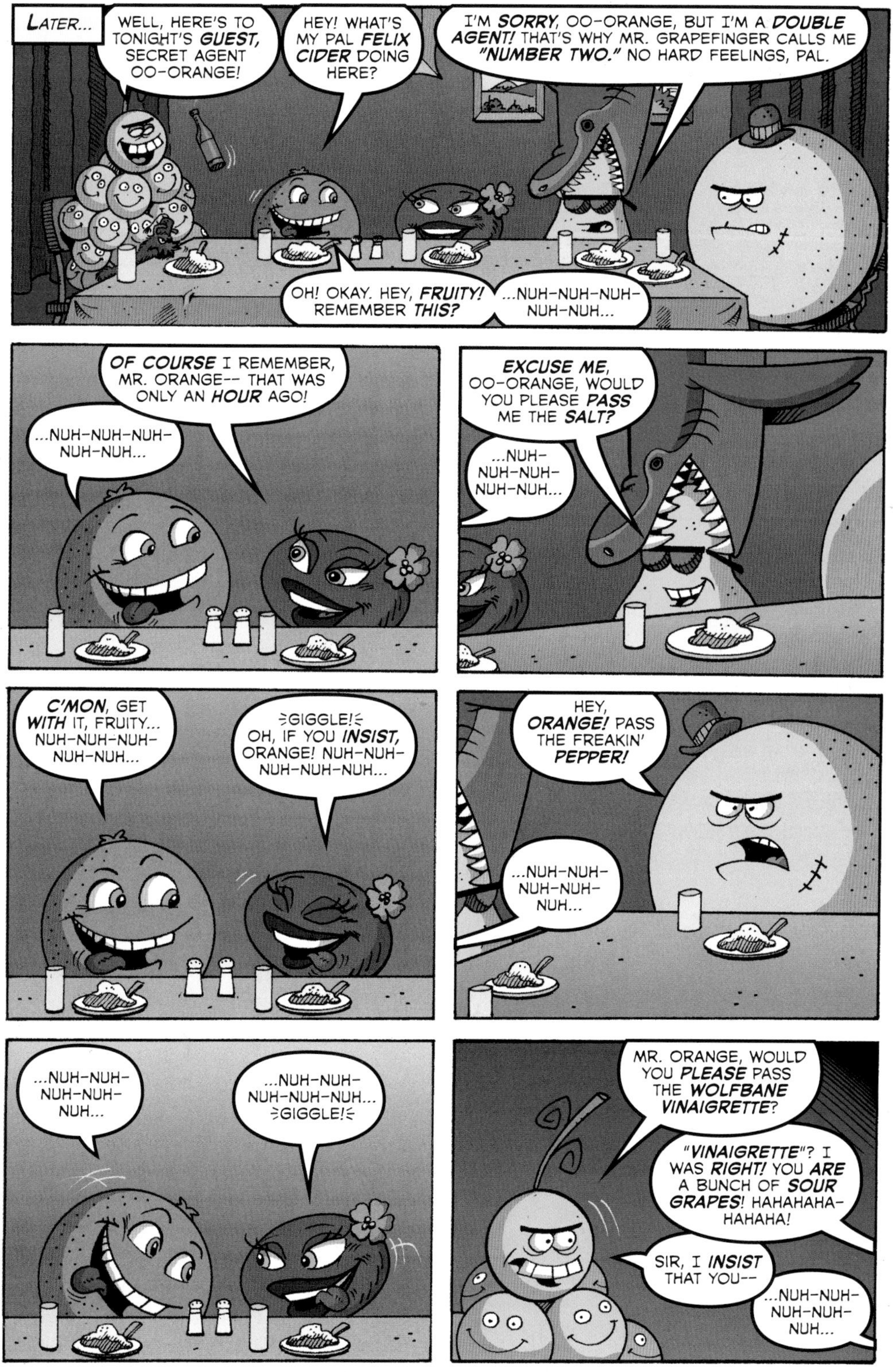
LATER...
WELL, HERE'S TO TONIGHT'S GUEST, SECRET AGENT OO-ORANGE!
HEY! WHAT'S MY PAL FELIX CIDER DOING HERE?
I'M SORRY, OO-ORANGE, BUT I'M A DOUBLE AGENT! THAT'S WHY MR. GRAPEFINGER CALLS ME "NUMBER TWO." NO HARD FEELINGS, PAL.
OH! OKAY. HEY, FRUITY! REMEMBER THIS?
...NUH-NUH-NUH-NUH-NUH...
OF COURSE I REMEMBER, MR. ORANGE-- THAT WAS ONLY AN HOUR AGO!
...NUH-NUH-NUH-NUH-NUH...
EXCUSE ME, OO-ORANGE, WOULD YOU PLEASE PASS ME THE SALT?
...NUH-NUH-NUH-NUH-NUH...
C'MON, GET WITH IT, FRUITY... NUH-NUH-NUH-NUH-NUH...
⋛GIGGLE!⋚ OH, IF YOU INSIST, ORANGE! NUH-NUH-NUH-NUH-NUH...
HEY, ORANGE! PASS THE FREAKIN' PEPPER!
...NUH-NUH-NUH-NUH-NUH...
...NUH-NUH-NUH-NUH-NUH...
...NUH-NUH-NUH-NUH-NUH... ⋛GIGGLE!⋚
MR. ORANGE, WOULD YOU PLEASE PASS THE WOLFBANE VINAIGRETTE?
"VINAIGRETTE"? I WAS RIGHT! YOU ARE A BUNCH OF SOUR GRAPES! HAHAHAHA-HAHAHA!
SIR, I INSIST THAT YOU--
...NUH-NUH-NUH-NUH-NUH...

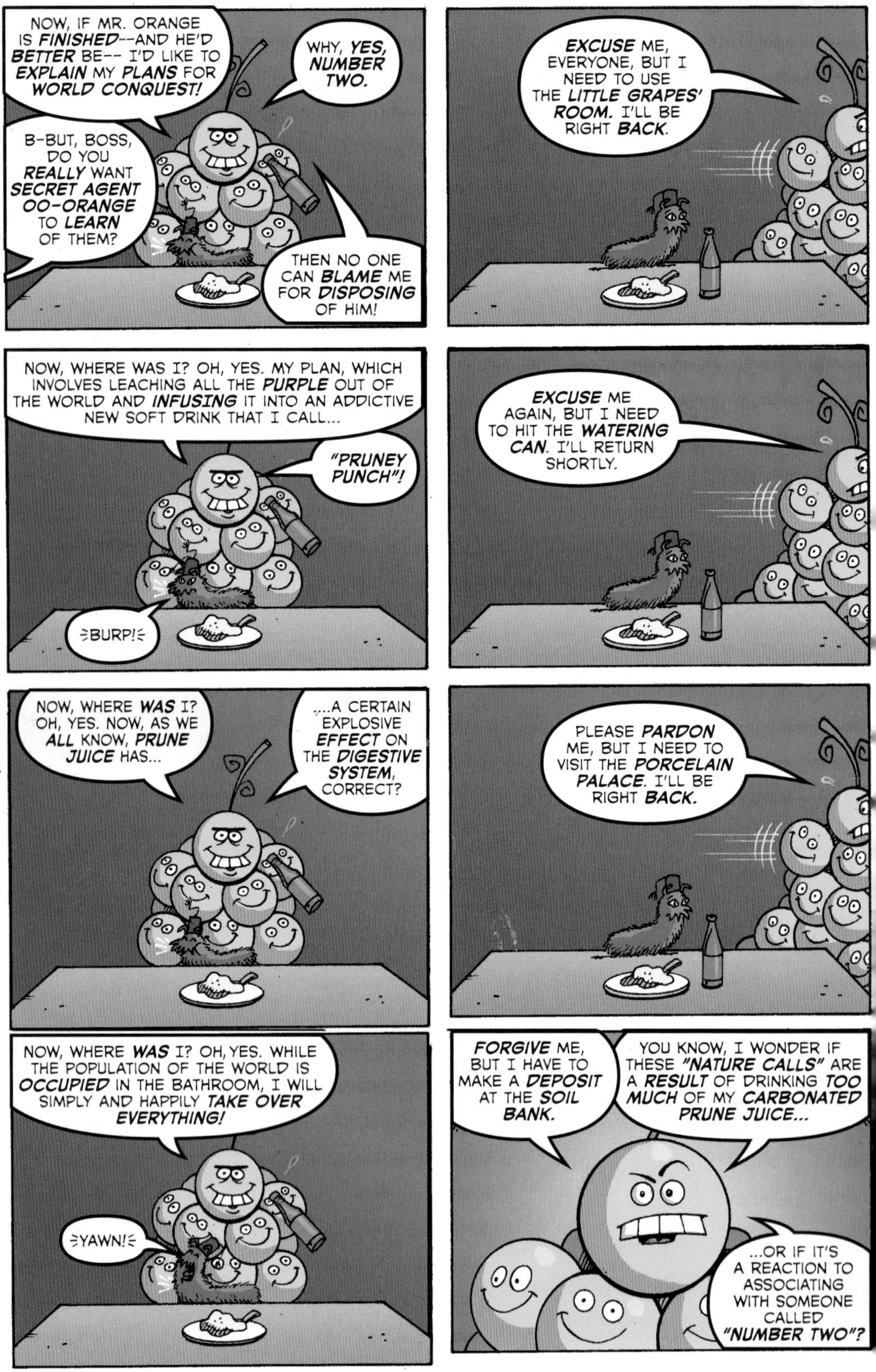
NOW, IF MR. ORANGE IS FINISHED--AND HE'D BETTER BE-- I'D LIKE TO EXPLAIN MY PLANS FOR WORLD CONQUEST!
WHY, YES, NUMBER TWO.
B-BUT, BOSS, DO YOU REALLY WANT SECRET AGENT OO-ORANGE TO LEARN OF THEM?
THEN NO ONE CAN BLAME ME FOR DISPOSING OF HIM!
EXCUSE ME, EVERYONE, BUT I NEED TO USE THE LITTLE GRAPES' ROOM. I'LL BE RIGHT BACK.
NOW, WHERE WAS I? OH, YES. MY PLAN, WHICH INVOLVES LEACHING ALL THE PURPLE OUT OF THE WORLD AND INFUSING IT INTO AN ADDICTIVE NEW SOFT DRINK THAT I CALL...
"PRUNEY PUNCH"!
BURP!
EXCUSE ME AGAIN, BUT I NEED TO HIT THE WATERING CAN. I'LL RETURN SHORTLY.
NOW, WHERE WAS I? OH, YES. NOW, AS WE ALL KNOW, PRUNE JUICE HAS...
...A CERTAIN EXPLOSIVE EFFECT ON THE DIGESTIVE SYSTEM, CORRECT?
PLEASE PARDON ME, BUT I NEED TO VISIT THE PORCELAIN PALACE. I'LL BE RIGHT BACK.
NOW, WHERE WAS I? OH, YES. WHILE THE POPULATION OF THE WORLD IS OCCUPIED IN THE BATHROOM, I WILL SIMPLY AND HAPPILY TAKE OVER EVERYTHING!
YAWN!
FORGIVE ME, BUT I HAVE TO MAKE A DEPOSIT AT THE SOIL BANK.
YOU KNOW, I WONDER IF THESE "NATURE CALLS" ARE A RESULT OF DRINKING TOO MUCH OF MY CARBONATED PRUNE JUICE...
...OR IF IT'S A REACTION TO ASSOCIATING WITH SOMEONE CALLED "NUMBER TWO"?

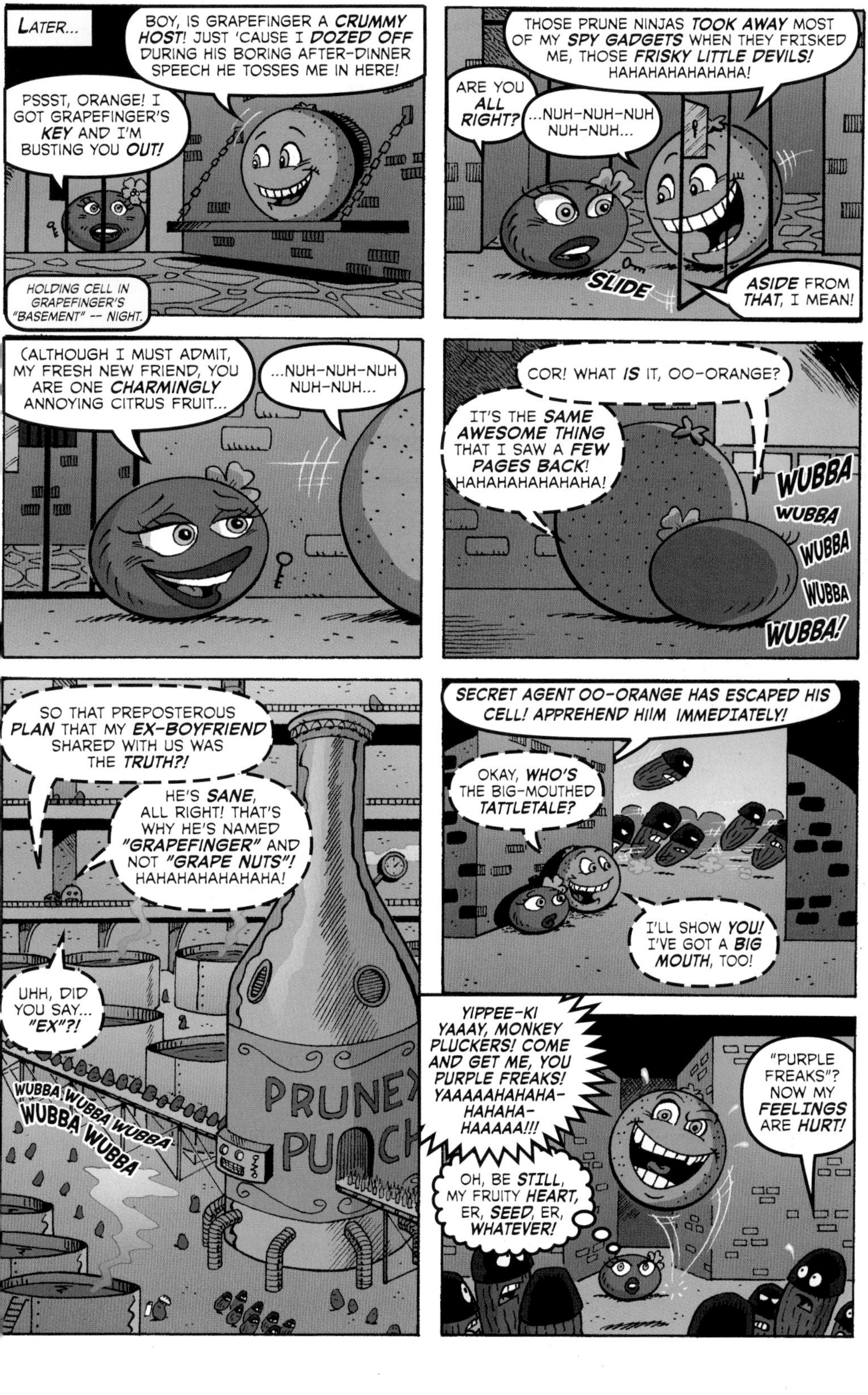
LATER...
BOY, IS GRAPEFINGER A CRUMMY HOST! JUST 'CAUSE I DOZED OFF DURING HIS BORING AFTER-DINNER SPEECH HE TOSSES ME IN HERE!
PSSST, ORANGE! I GOT GRAPEFINGER'S KEY AND I'M BUSTING YOU OUT!
HOLDING CELL IN GRAPEFINGER'S "BASEMENT" -- NIGHT.
THOSE PRUNE NINJAS TOOK AWAY MOST OF MY SPY GADGETS WHEN THEY FRISKED ME, THOSE FRISKY LITTLE DEVILS! HAHAHAHAHAHAHA!
ARE YOU ALL RIGHT?
...NUH-NUH-NUH NUH-NUH...
SLIDE
ASIDE FROM THAT, I MEAN!
(ALTHOUGH I MUST ADMIT, MY FRESH NEW FRIEND, YOU ARE ONE CHARMINGLY ANNOYING CITRUS FRUIT...
...NUH-NUH-NUH NUH-NUH...
COR! WHAT IS IT, OO-ORANGE?
IT'S THE SAME AWESOME THING THAT I SAW A FEW PAGES BACK! HAHAHAHAHAHAHA!
WUBBA WUBBA WUBBA WUBBA WUBBA!
SO THAT PREPOSTEROUS PLAN THAT MY EX-BOYFRIEND SHARED WITH US WAS THE TRUTH?!
HE'S SANE, ALL RIGHT! THAT'S WHY HE'S NAMED "GRAPEFINGER" AND NOT "GRAPE NUTS"! HAHAHAHAHAHAHA!
UHH, DID YOU SAY... "EX"?!
WUBBA WUBBA WUBBA
WUBBA WUBBA
PRUNEX PUNCH
SECRET AGENT OO-ORANGE HAS ESCAPED HIS CELL! APPREHEND HIIM IMMEDIATELY!
OKAY, WHO'S THE BIG-MOUTHED TATTLETALE?
I'LL SHOW YOU! I'VE GOT A BIG MOUTH, TOO!
YIPPEE-KI YAAAY, MONKEY PLUCKERS! COME AND GET ME, YOU PURPLE FREAKS! YAAAAAHAHAHA-HAHAHA-HAAAAA!!!
"PURPLE FREAKS"? NOW MY FEELINGS ARE HURT!
OH, BE STILL, MY FRUITY HEART, ER, SEED, ER, WHATEVER!

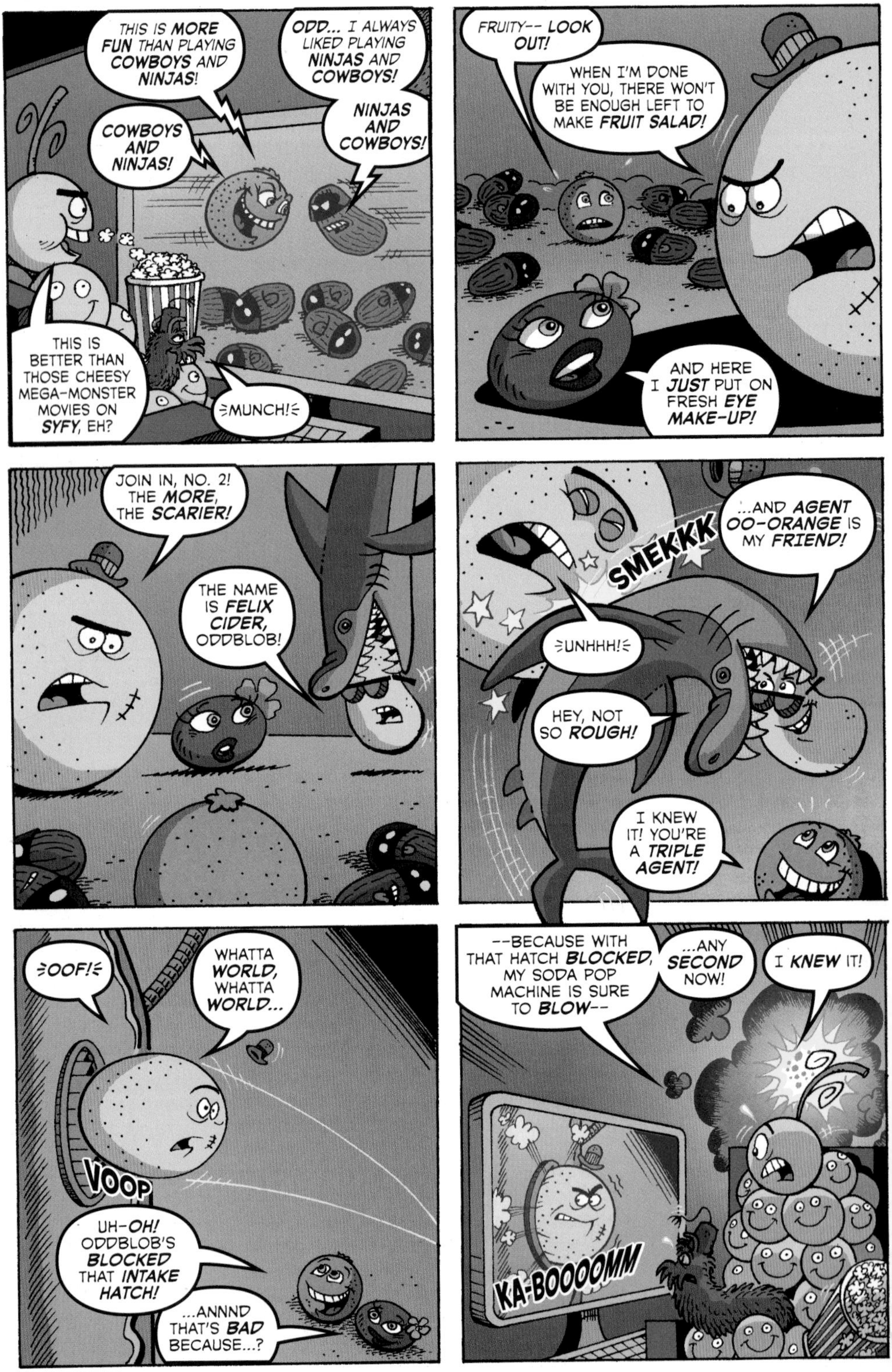
THIS IS MORE FUN THAN PLAYING COWBOYS AND NINJAS!
ODD... I ALWAYS LIKED PLAYING NINJAS AND COWBOYS!
COWBOYS AND NINJAS!
NINJAS AND COWBOYS!
THIS IS BETTER THAN THOSE CHEESY MEGA-MONSTER MOVIES ON SYFY, EH?
MUNCH!
FRUITY-- LOOK OUT!
WHEN I'M DONE WITH YOU, THERE WON'T BE ENOUGH LEFT TO MAKE FRUIT SALAD!
AND HERE I JUST PUT ON FRESH EYE MAKE-UP!
JOIN IN, NO. 2! THE MORE, THE SCARIER!
THE NAME IS FELIX CIDER, ODDBLOB!
...AND AGENT OO-ORANGE IS MY FRIEND!
SMEKKK
UNHHH!
HEY, NOT SO ROUGH!
I KNEW IT! YOU'RE A TRIPLE AGENT!
OOF!
WHATTA WORLD, WHATTA WORLD...
VOOP
UH-OH! ODDBLOB'S BLOCKED THAT INTAKE HATCH!
...ANNND THAT'S BAD BECAUSE...?
--BECAUSE WITH THAT HATCH BLOCKED, MY SODA POP MACHINE IS SURE TO BLOW--
...ANY SECOND NOW!
I KNEW IT!
KA-BOOOOMM

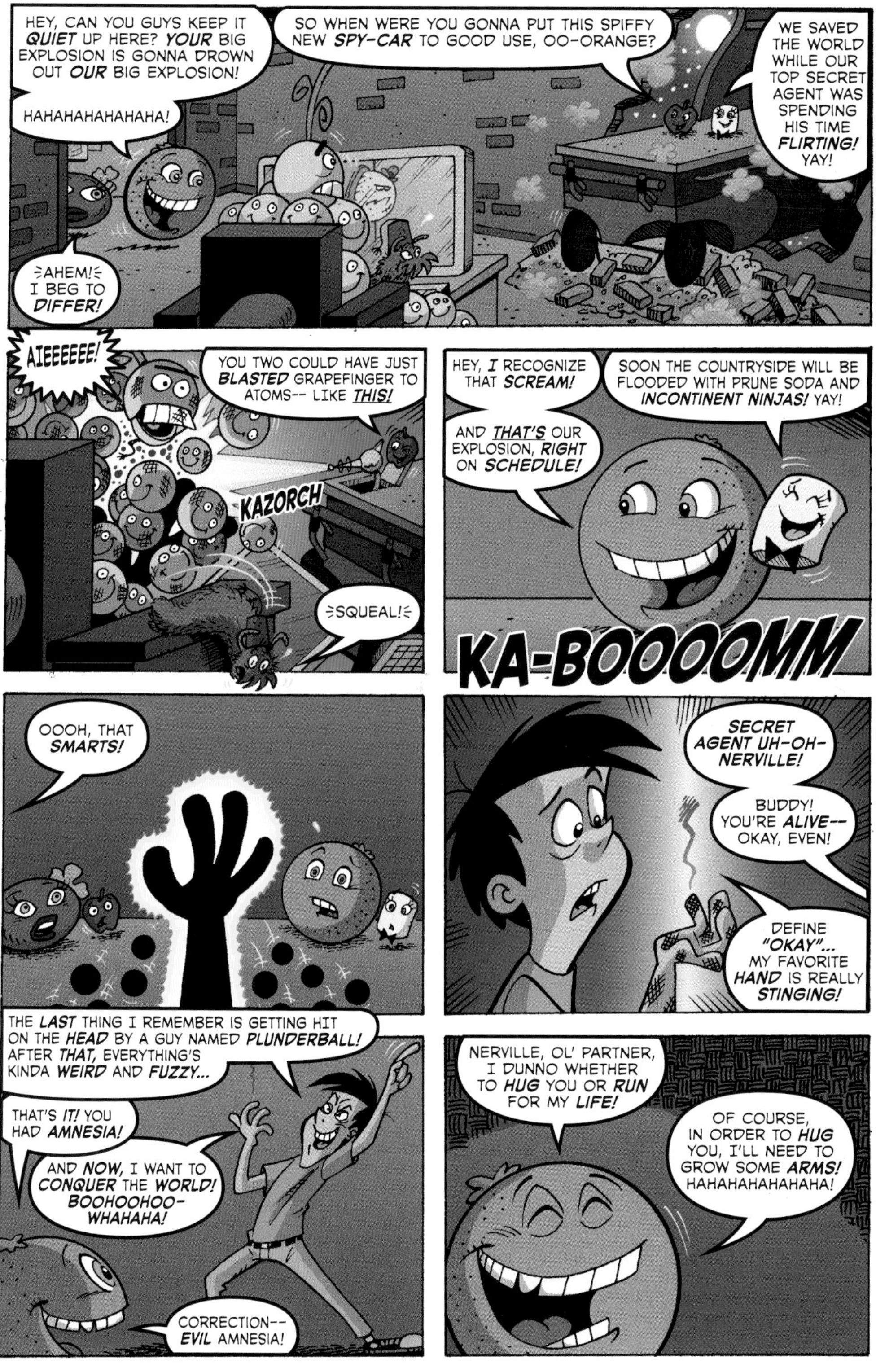
HEY, CAN YOU GUYS KEEP IT QUIET UP HERE? YOUR BIG EXPLOSION IS GONNA DROWN OUT OUR BIG EXPLOSION!
HAHAHAHAHAHAHA!
SO WHEN WERE YOU GONNA PUT THIS SPIFFY NEW SPY-CAR TO GOOD USE, OO-ORANGE?
WE SAVED THE WORLD WHILE OUR TOP SECRET AGENT WAS SPENDING HIS TIME FLIRTING! YAY!
AHEM! I BEG TO DIFFER!
AIEEEEEE!
YOU TWO COULD HAVE JUST BLASTED GRAPEFINGER TO ATOMS-- LIKE THIS!
KAZORCH
SQUEAL!
HEY, I RECOGNIZE THAT SCREAM!
SOON THE COUNTRYSIDE WILL BE FLOODED WITH PRUNE SODA AND INCONTINENT NINJAS! YAY!
AND THAT'S OUR EXPLOSION, RIGHT ON SCHEDULE!
KA-BOOOOMM
OOOH, THAT SMARTS!
SECRET AGENT UH-OH-NERVILLE!
BUDDY! YOU'RE ALIVE-- OKAY, EVEN!
DEFINE "OKAY"... MY FAVORITE HAND IS REALLY STINGING!
THE LAST THING I REMEMBER IS GETTING HIT ON THE HEAD BY A GUY NAMED PLUNDERBALL! AFTER THAT, EVERYTHING'S KINDA WEIRD AND FUZZY...
THAT'S IT! YOU HAD AMNESIA!
AND NOW, I WANT TO CONQUER THE WORLD! BOOHOOHOO-WHAHAHA!
CORRECTION-- EVIL AMNESIA!
NERVILLE, OL' PARTNER, I DUNNO WHETHER TO HUG YOU OR RUN FOR MY LIFE!
OF COURSE, IN ORDER TO HUG YOU, I'LL NEED TO GROW SOME ARMS! HAHAHAHAHAHAHA!

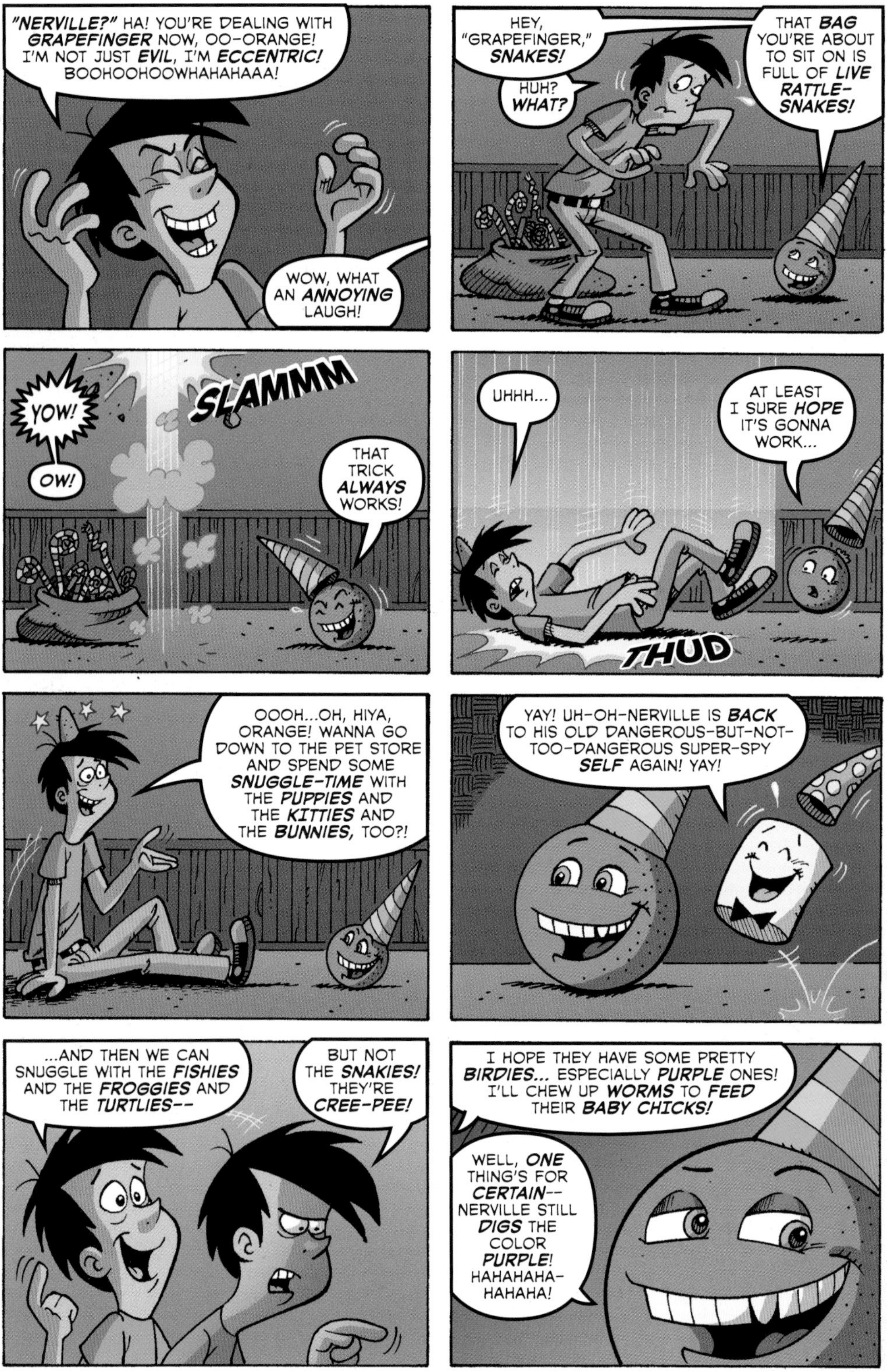
"NERVILLE?" HA! YOU'RE DEALING WITH GRAPEFINGER NOW, OO-ORANGE! I'M NOT JUST EVIL, I'M ECCENTRIC! BOOHOOHOOWHAHAHAAA!
WOW, WHAT AN ANNOYING LAUGH!
HEY, "GRAPEFINGER," SNAKES!
HUH? WHAT?
THAT BAG YOU'RE ABOUT TO SIT ON IS FULL OF LIVE RATTLE-SNAKES!
YOW!
OW!
SLAMMM
THAT TRICK ALWAYS WORKS!
UHHH...
AT LEAST I SURE HOPE IT'S GONNA WORK...
THUD
OOOH...OH, HIYA, ORANGE! WANNA GO DOWN TO THE PET STORE AND SPEND SOME SNUGGLE-TIME WITH THE PUPPIES AND THE KITTIES AND THE BUNNIES, TOO?!
YAY! UH-OH-NERVILLE IS BACK TO HIS OLD DANGEROUS-BUT-NOT-TOO-DANGEROUS SUPER-SPY SELF AGAIN! YAY!
...AND THEN WE CAN SNUGGLE WITH THE FISHIES AND THE FROGGIES AND THE TURTLIES--
BUT NOT THE SNAKIES! THEY'RE CREE-PEE!
I HOPE THEY HAVE SOME PRETTY BIRDIES... ESPECIALLY PURPLE ONES! I'LL CHEW UP WORMS TO FEED THEIR BABY CHICKS!
WELL, ONE THING'S FOR CERTAIN-- NERVILLE STILL DIGS THE COLOR PURPLE! HAHAHAHA-HAHAHA!

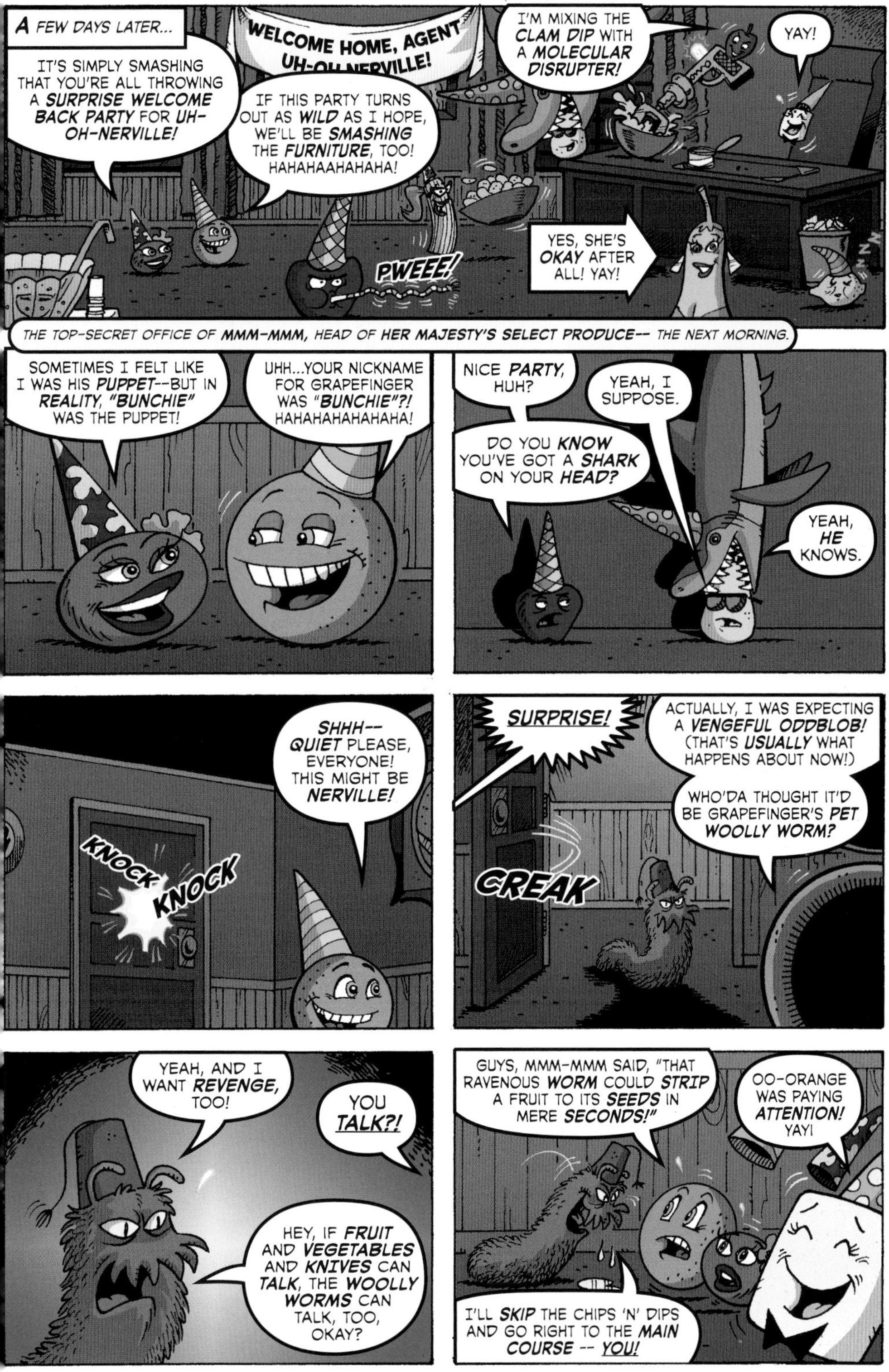
A FEW DAYS LATER...
WELCOME HOME, AGENT UH-OH NERVILLE!
IT'S SIMPLY SMASHING THAT YOU'RE ALL THROWING A SURPRISE WELCOME BACK PARTY FOR UH-OH-NERVILLE!
IF THIS PARTY TURNS OUT AS WILD AS I HOPE, WE'LL BE SMASHING THE FURNITURE, TOO! HAHAHAAAHAHAHA!
I'M MIXING THE CLAM DIP WITH A MOLECULAR DISRUPTER!
YAY!
PWEEE!
YES, SHE'S OKAY AFTER ALL! YAY!
THE TOP-SECRET OFFICE OF MMM-MMM, HEAD OF HER MAJESTY'S SELECT PRODUCE-- THE NEXT MORNING.
SOMETIMES I FELT LIKE I WAS HIS PUPPET--BUT IN REALITY, "BUNCHIE" WAS THE PUPPET!
UHH...YOUR NICKNAME FOR GRAPEFINGER WAS "BUNCHIE"?! HAHAHAHAHAHAHA!
NICE PARTY, HUH?
YEAH, I SUPPOSE.
DO YOU KNOW YOU'VE GOT A SHARK ON YOUR HEAD?
YEAH, HE KNOWS.
SHHH-- QUIET PLEASE, EVERYONE! THIS MIGHT BE NERVILLE!
KNOCK KNOCK
SURPRISE!
ACTUALLY, I WAS EXPECTING A VENGEFUL ODDBLOB! (THAT'S USUALLY WHAT HAPPENS ABOUT NOW!)
WHO'DA THOUGHT IT'D BE GRAPEFINGER'S PET WOOLLY WORM?
CREAK
YEAH, AND I WANT REVENGE, TOO!
YOU TALK?!
HEY, IF FRUIT AND VEGETABLES AND KNIVES CAN TALK, THE WOOLLY WORMS CAN TALK, TOO, OKAY?
GUYS, MMM-MMM SAID, "THAT RAVENOUS WORM COULD STRIP A FRUIT TO ITS SEEDS IN MERE SECONDS!"
OO-ORANGE WAS PAYING ATTENTION! YAY!
I'LL SKIP THE CHIPS 'N' DIPS AND GO RIGHT TO THE MAIN COURSE -- YOU!

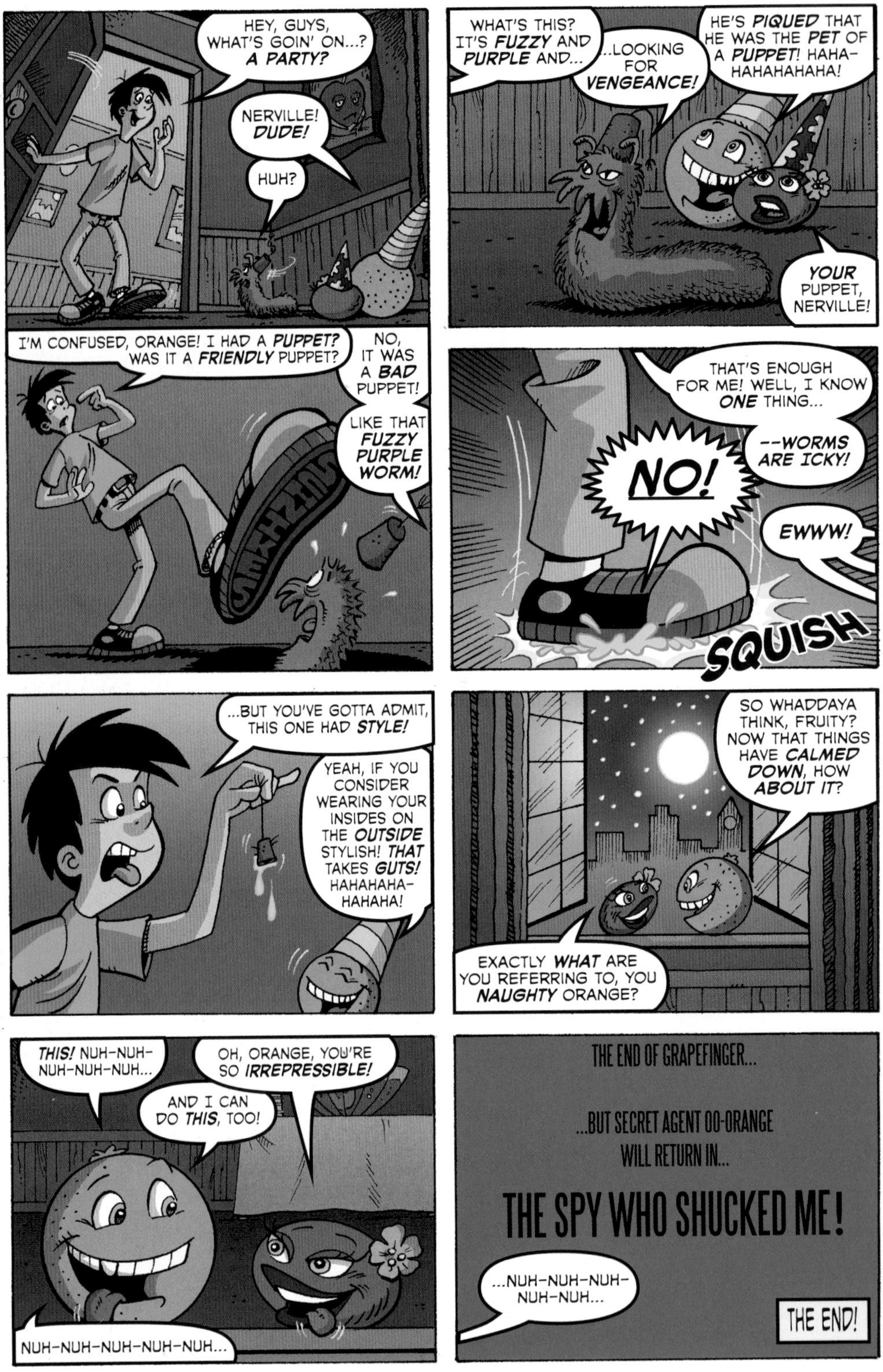
HEY, GUYS, WHAT'S GOIN' ON...? A PARTY?
NERVILLE! DUDE!
HUH?
WHAT'S THIS? IT'S FUZZY AND PURPLE AND...
...LOOKING FOR VENGEANCE!
HE'S PIQUED THAT HE WAS THE PET OF A PUPPET! HAHA-HAHAHAHAHA!
YOUR PUPPET, NERVILLE!
I'M CONFUSED, ORANGE! I HAD A PUPPET? WAS IT A FRIENDLY PUPPET?
NO, IT WAS A BAD PUPPET!
LIKE THAT FUZZY PURPLE WORM!
THAT'S ENOUGH FOR ME! WELL, I KNOW ONE THING...
--WORMS ARE ICKY!
NO!
EWWW!
SQUISH
...BUT YOU'VE GOTTA ADMIT, THIS ONE HAD STYLE!
YEAH, IF YOU CONSIDER WEARING YOUR INSIDES ON THE OUTSIDE STYLISH! THAT TAKES GUTS! HAHAHAHA-HAHAHA!
SO WHADDAYA THINK, FRUITY? NOW THAT THINGS HAVE CALMED DOWN, HOW ABOUT IT?
EXACTLY WHAT ARE YOU REFERRING TO, YOU NAUGHTY ORANGE?
THIS! NUH-NUH-NUH-NUH-NUH-NUH-NUH-NUH...
OH, ORANGE, YOU'RE SO IRREPRESSIBLE!
AND I CAN DO THIS, TOO!
NUH-NUH-NUH-NUH-NUH...
THE END OF GRAPEFINGER...
...BUT SECRET AGENT 00-ORANGE WILL RETURN IN...
THE SPY WHO SHUCKED ME!
...NUH-NUH-NUH-NUH-NUH-NUH-NUH...
THE END!

PLUM'S DAY OUT

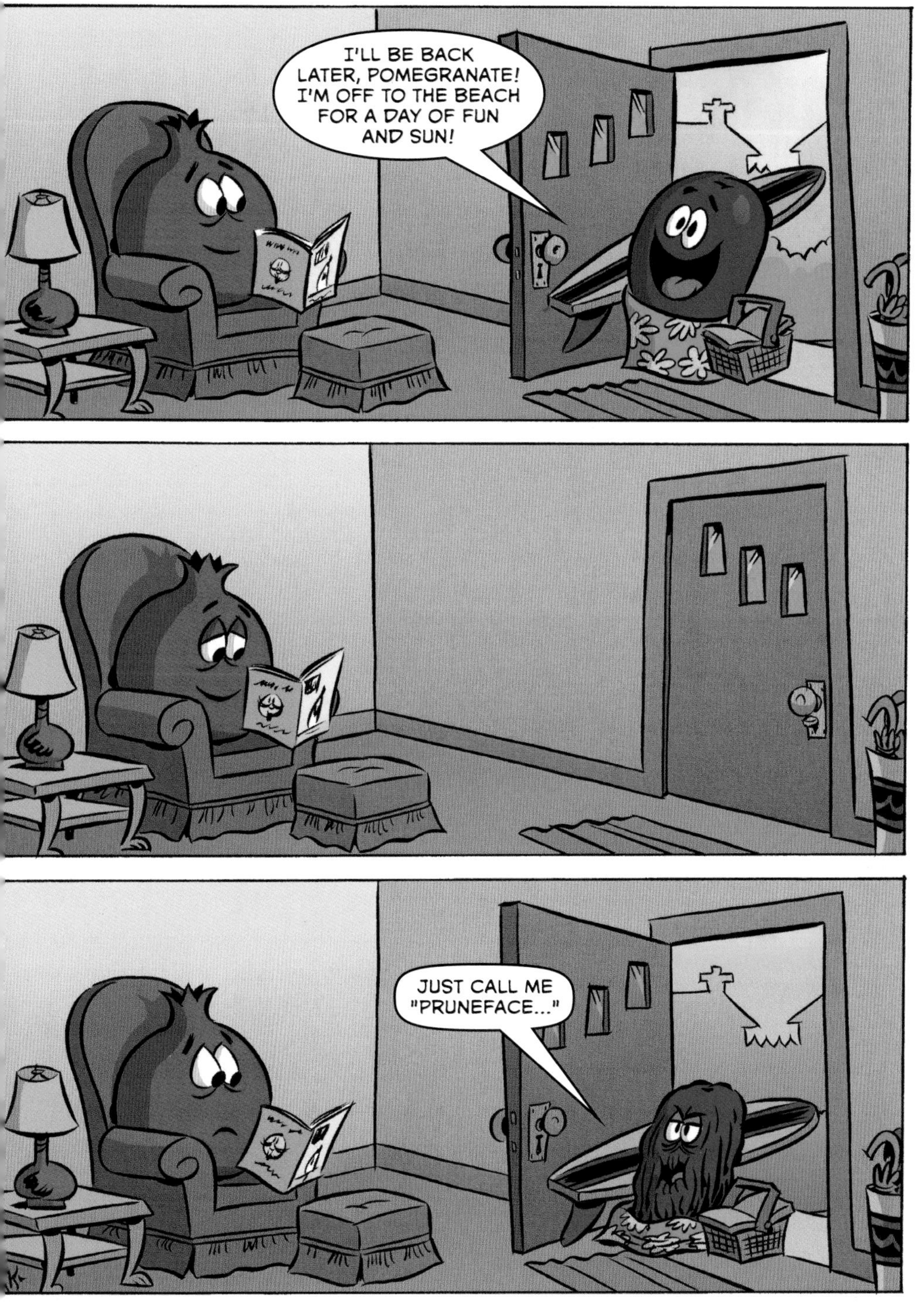
I'LL BE BACK LATER, POMEGRANATE! I'M OFF TO THE BEACH FOR A DAY OF FUN AND SUN!
JUST CALL ME "PRUNEFACE..."

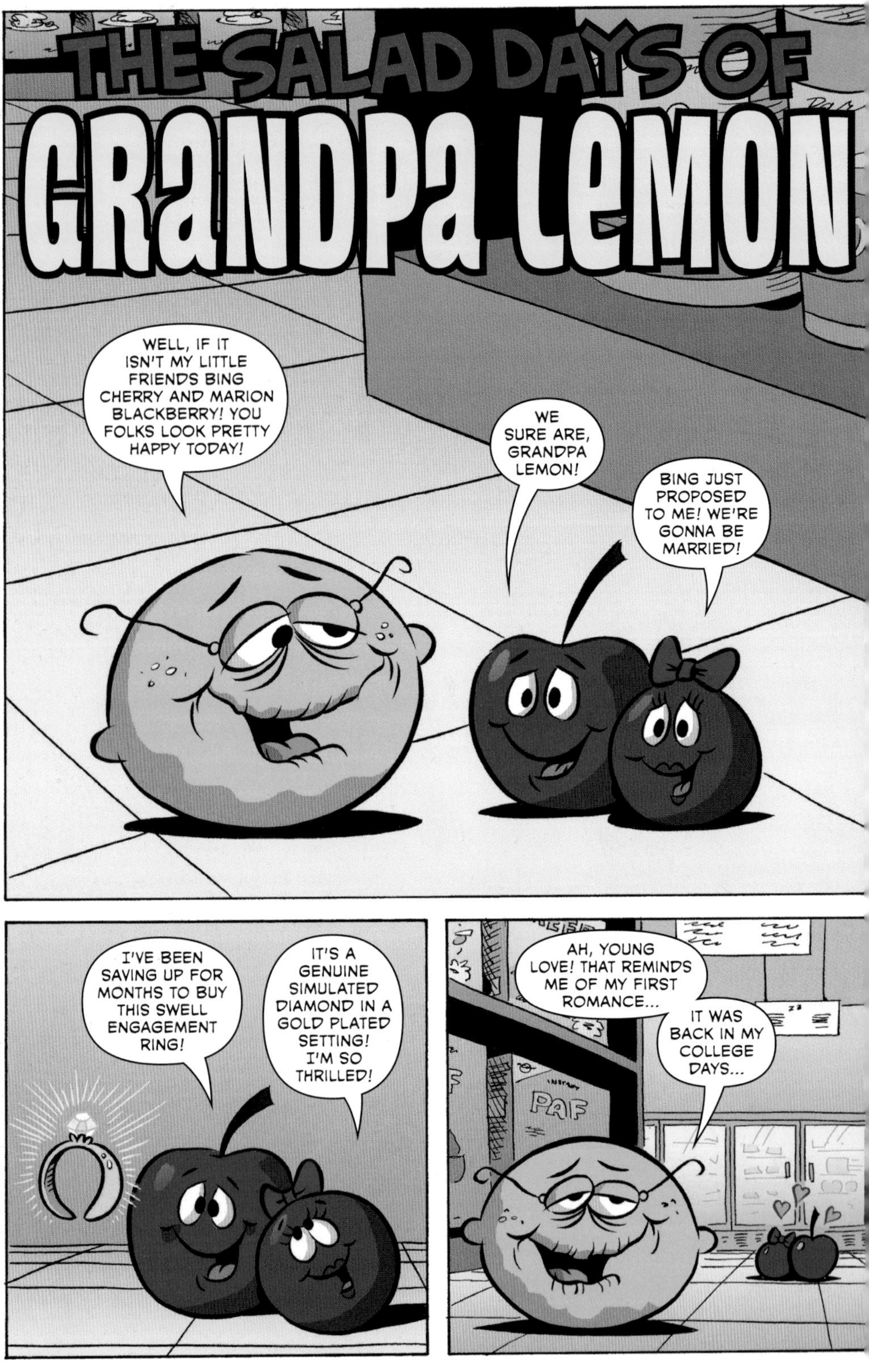
THE SALAD DAYS OF
GRANDPA LEMON
WELL, IF IT ISN'T MY LITTLE FRIENDS BING CHERRY AND MARION BLACKBERRY! YOU FOLKS LOOK PRETTY HAPPY TODAY!
WE SURE ARE, GRANDPA LEMON!
BING JUST PROPOSED TO ME! WE'RE GONNA BE MARRIED!
I'VE BEEN SAVING UP FOR MONTHS TO BUY THIS SWELL ENGAGEMENT RING!
IT'S A GENUINE SIMULATED DIAMOND IN A GOLD PLATED SETTING! I'M SO THRILLED!
AH, YOUNG LOVE! THAT REMINDS ME OF MY FIRST ROMANCE...
IT WAS BACK IN MY COLLEGE DAYS...
PAF

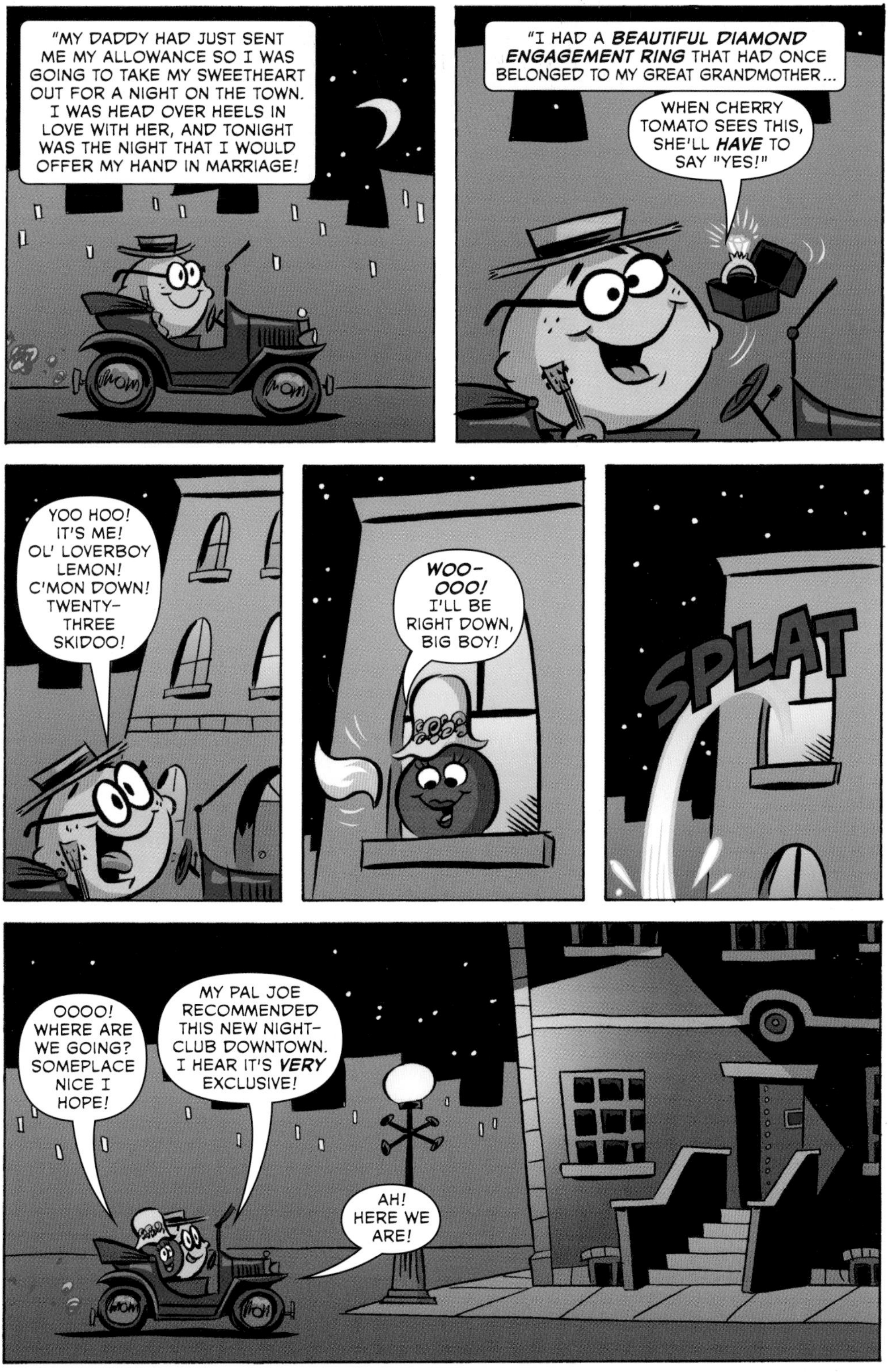
"MY DADDY HAD JUST SENT ME MY ALLOWANCE SO I WAS GOING TO TAKE MY SWEETHEART OUT FOR A NIGHT ON THE TOWN. I WAS HEAD OVER HEELS IN LOVE WITH HER, AND TONIGHT WAS THE NIGHT THAT I WOULD OFFER MY HAND IN MARRIAGE!
"I HAD A BEAUTIFUL DIAMOND ENGAGEMENT RING THAT HAD ONCE BELONGED TO MY GREAT GRANDMOTHER...
WHEN CHERRY TOMATO SEES THIS, SHE'LL HAVE TO SAY "YES!"
YOO HOO! IT'S ME! OL' LOVERBOY LEMON! C'MON DOWN! TWENTY-THREE SKIDOO!
WOO-OOO! I'LL BE RIGHT DOWN, BIG BOY!
SPLAT
OOOO! WHERE ARE WE GOING? SOMEPLACE NICE I HOPE!
MY PAL JOE RECOMMENDED THIS NEW NIGHT-CLUB DOWNTOWN. I HEAR IT'S VERY EXCLUSIVE!
AH! HERE WE ARE!

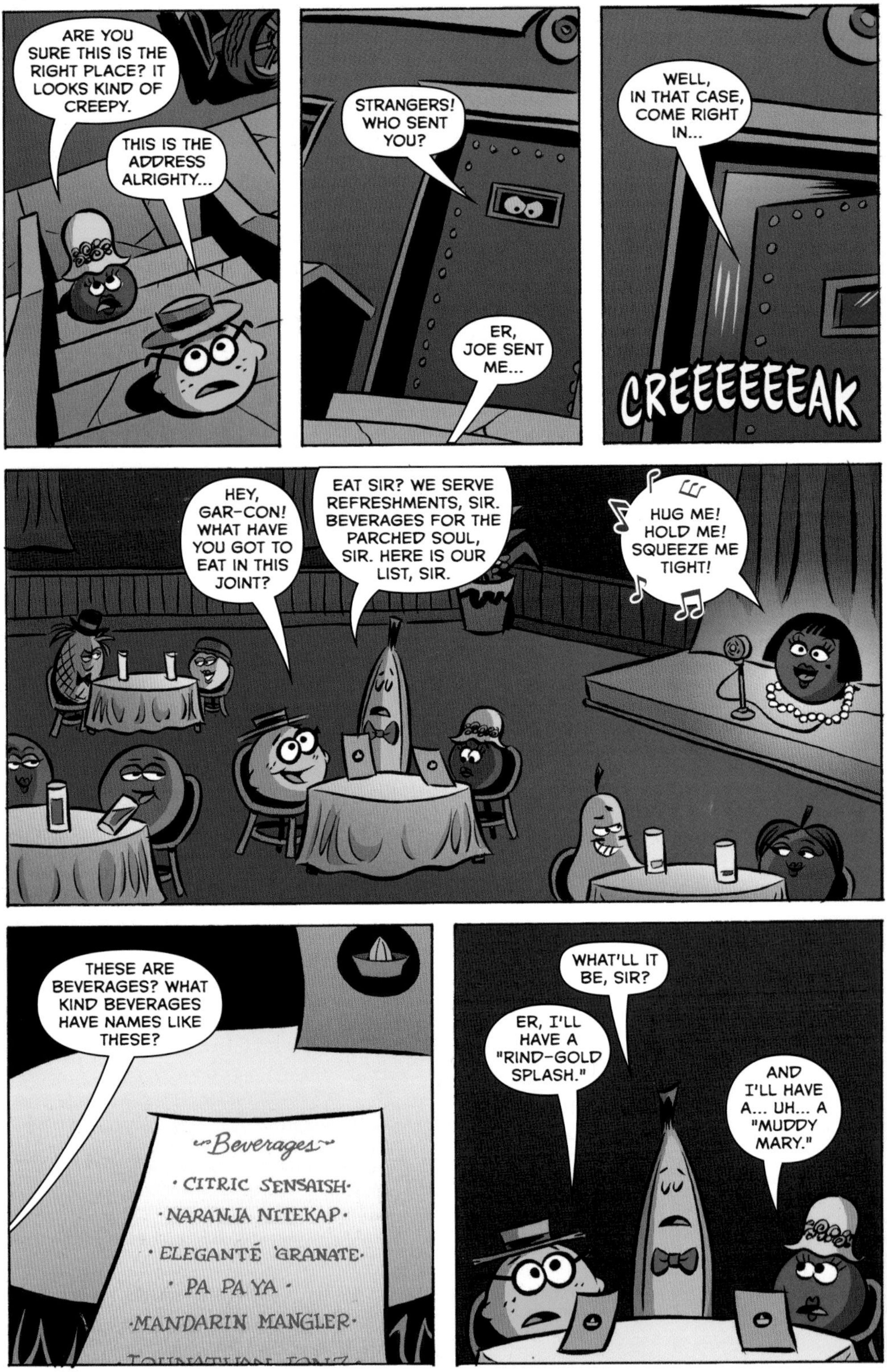
ARE YOU SURE THIS IS THE RIGHT PLACE? IT LOOKS KIND OF CREEPY.
THIS IS THE ADDRESS ALRIGHTY...
STRANGERS! WHO SENT YOU?
ER, JOE SENT ME...
WELL, IN THAT CASE, COME RIGHT IN...
CREEEEEEAK
HEY, GAR-CON! WHAT HAVE YOU GOT TO EAT IN THIS JOINT?
EAT SIR? WE SERVE REFRESHMENTS, SIR. BEVERAGES FOR THE PARCHED SOUL, SIR. HERE IS OUR LIST, SIR.
HUG ME! HOLD ME! SQUEEZE ME TIGHT!
THESE ARE BEVERAGES? WHAT KIND BEVERAGES HAVE NAMES LIKE THESE?
Beverages
· CITRIC SENSAISH ·
· NARANJA NITEKAP ·
· ELEGANTÉ 'GRANATE ·
· PA PA YA ·
· MANDARIN MANGLER ·
WHAT'LL IT BE, SIR?
ER, I'LL HAVE A "RIND-GOLD SPLASH."
AND I'LL HAVE A... UH... A "MUDDY MARY."

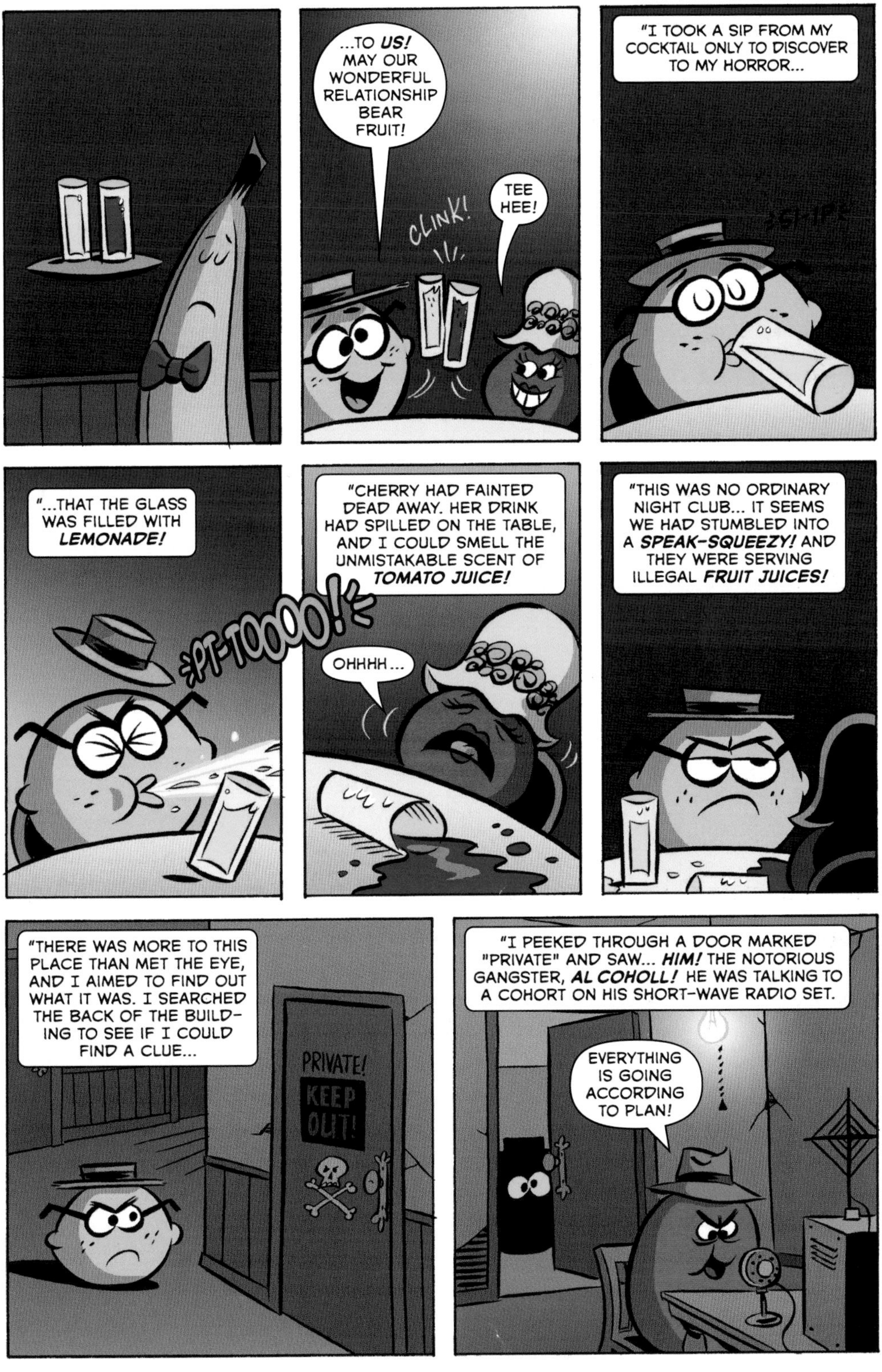
...TO US! MAY OUR WONDERFUL RELATIONSHIP BEAR FRUIT!
CLINK!
TEE HEE!
"I TOOK A SIP FROM MY COCKTAIL ONLY TO DISCOVER TO MY HORROR...
"...THAT THE GLASS WAS FILLED WITH LEMONADE!
PT-TOOOO!
"CHERRY HAD FAINTED DEAD AWAY. HER DRINK HAD SPILLED ON THE TABLE, AND I COULD SMELL THE UNMISTAKABLE SCENT OF TOMATO JUICE!
OHHHH...
"THIS WAS NO ORDINARY NIGHT CLUB... IT SEEMS WE HAD STUMBLED INTO A SPEAK-SQUEEZY! AND THEY WERE SERVING ILLEGAL FRUIT JUICES!
"THERE WAS MORE TO THIS PLACE THAN MET THE EYE, AND I AIMED TO FIND OUT WHAT IT WAS. I SEARCHED THE BACK OF THE BUILDING TO SEE IF I COULD FIND A CLUE...
PRIVATE!
KEEP OUT!
"I PEEKED THROUGH A DOOR MARKED "PRIVATE" AND SAW... HIM! THE NOTORIOUS GANGSTER, AL COHOLL! HE WAS TALKING TO A COHORT ON HIS SHORT-WAVE RADIO SET.
EVERYTHING IS GOING ACCORDING TO PLAN!

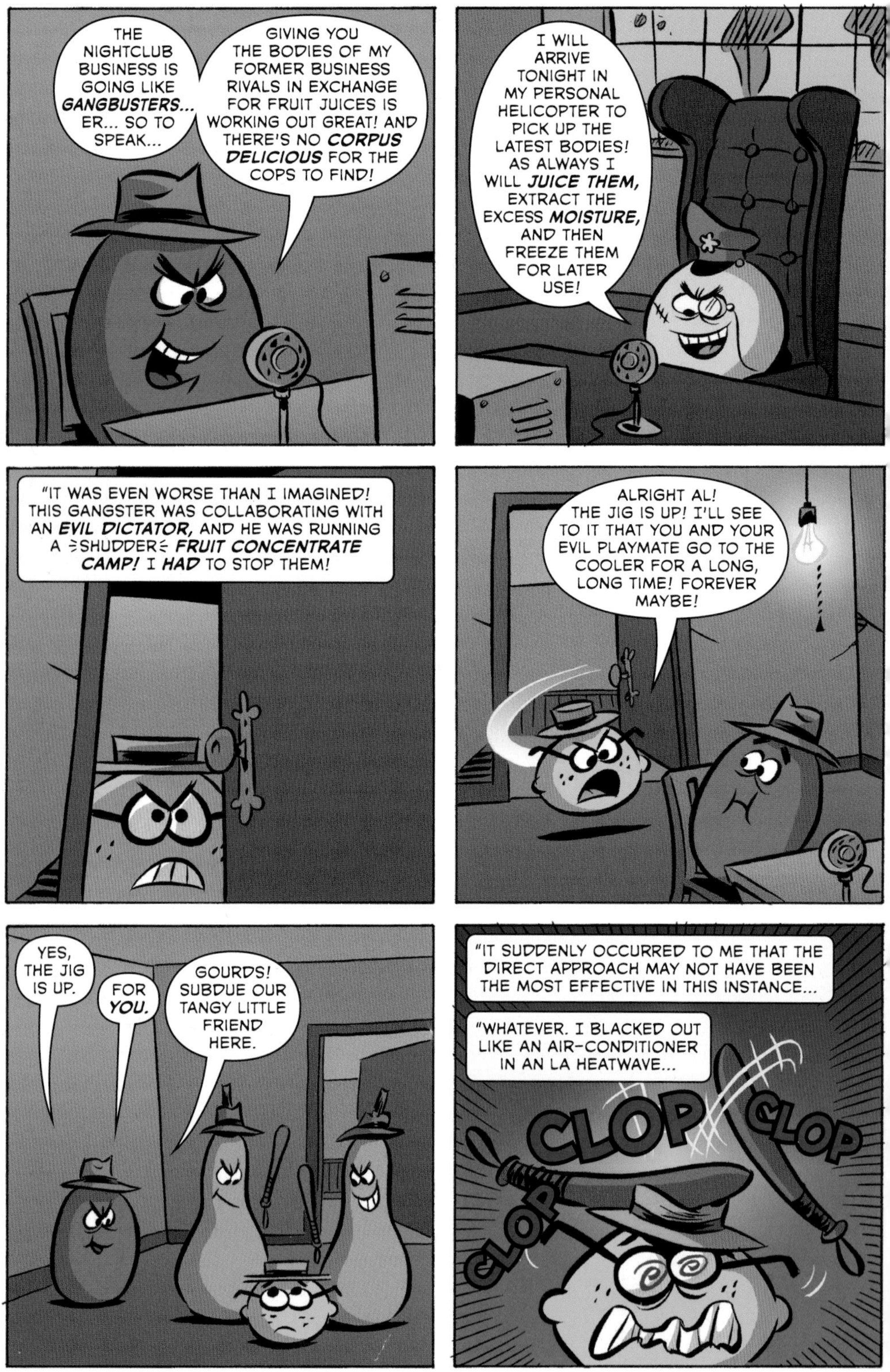
THE NIGHTCLUB BUSINESS IS GOING LIKE GANGBUSTERS... ER... SO TO SPEAK...
GIVING YOU THE BODIES OF MY FORMER BUSINESS RIVALS IN EXCHANGE FOR FRUIT JUICES IS WORKING OUT GREAT! AND THERE'S NO CORPUS DELICIOUS FOR THE COPS TO FIND!
I WILL ARRIVE TONIGHT IN MY PERSONAL HELICOPTER TO PICK UP THE LATEST BODIES! AS ALWAYS I WILL JUICE THEM, EXTRACT THE EXCESS MOISTURE, AND THEN FREEZE THEM FOR LATER USE!
"IT WAS EVEN WORSE THAN I IMAGINED! THIS GANGSTER WAS COLLABORATING WITH AN EVIL DICTATOR, AND HE WAS RUNNING A ≥SHUDDER≤ FRUIT CONCENTRATE CAMP! I HAD TO STOP THEM!
ALRIGHT AL! THE JIG IS UP! I'LL SEE TO IT THAT YOU AND YOUR EVIL PLAYMATE GO TO THE COOLER FOR A LONG, LONG TIME! FOREVER MAYBE!
YES, THE JIG IS UP.
FOR YOU.
GOURDS! SUBDUE OUR TANGY LITTLE FRIEND HERE.
"IT SUDDENLY OCCURRED TO ME THAT THE DIRECT APPROACH MAY NOT HAVE BEEN THE MOST EFFECTIVE IN THIS INSTANCE...
"WHATEVER. I BLACKED OUT LIKE AN AIR-CONDITIONER IN AN LA HEATWAVE...
CLOP
CLOP
CLOP
CLOP

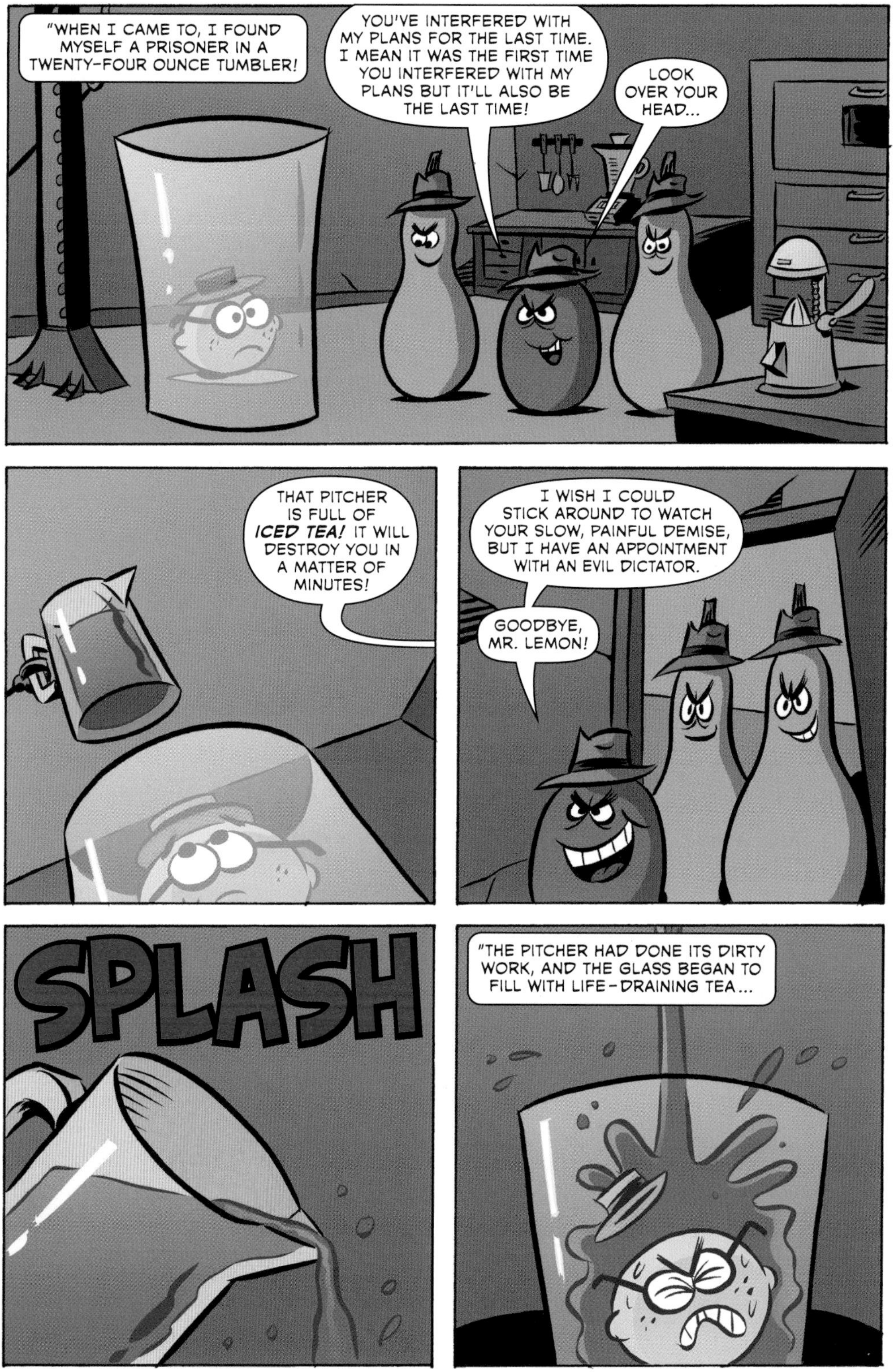
"WHEN I CAME TO, I FOUND MYSELF A PRISONER IN A TWENTY-FOUR OUNCE TUMBLER!
YOU'VE INTERFERED WITH MY PLANS FOR THE LAST TIME. I MEAN IT WAS THE FIRST TIME YOU INTERFERED WITH MY PLANS BUT IT'LL ALSO BE THE LAST TIME!
LOOK OVER YOUR HEAD...
THAT PITCHER IS FULL OF ICED TEA! IT WILL DESTROY YOU IN A MATTER OF MINUTES!
I WISH I COULD STICK AROUND TO WATCH YOUR SLOW, PAINFUL DEMISE, BUT I HAVE AN APPOINTMENT WITH AN EVIL DICTATOR.
GOODBYE, MR. LEMON!
SPLASH
"THE PITCHER HAD DONE ITS DIRTY WORK, AND THE GLASS BEGAN TO FILL WITH LIFE-DRAINING TEA...

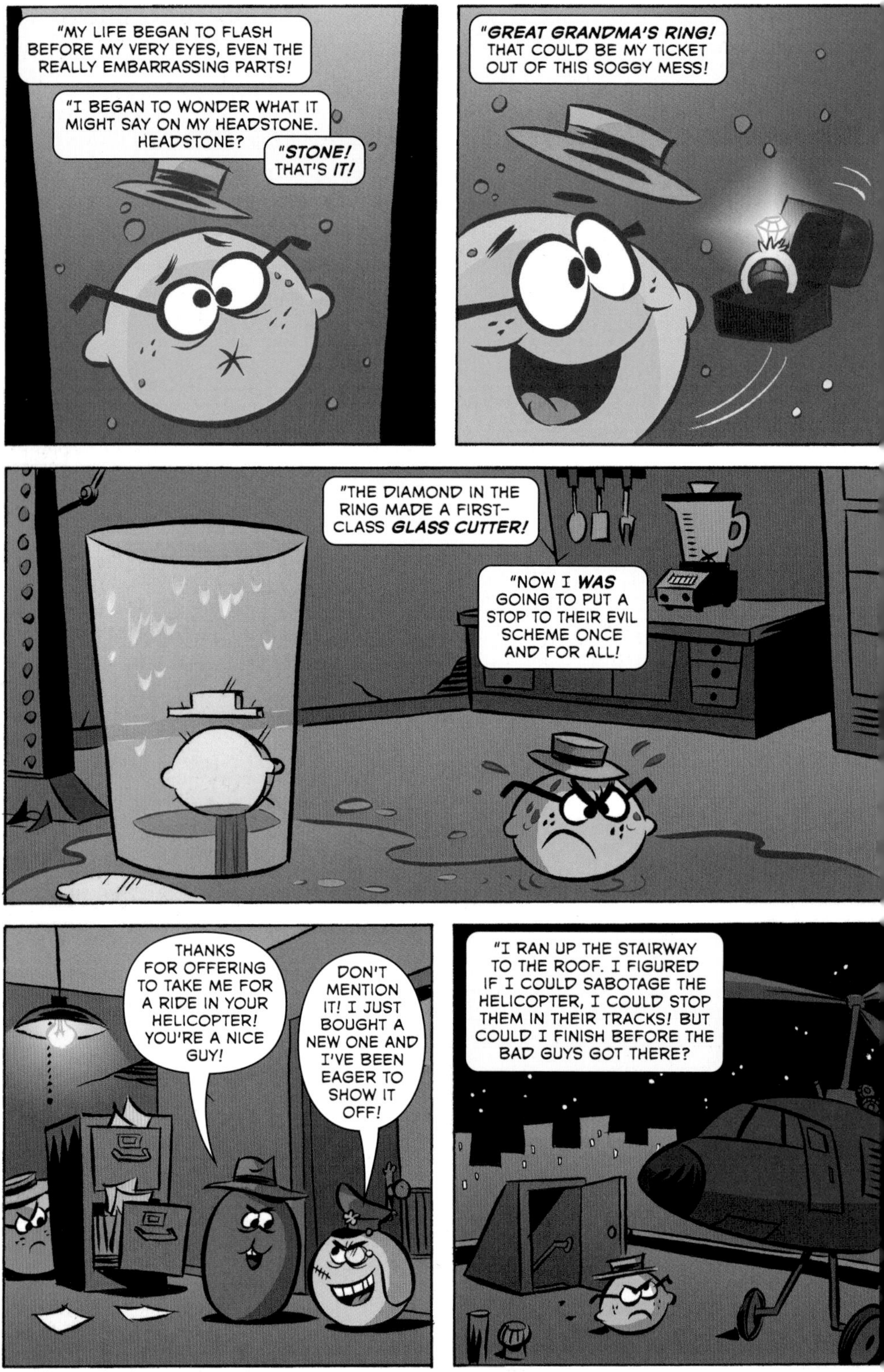
"MY LIFE BEGAN TO FLASH BEFORE MY VERY EYES, EVEN THE REALLY EMBARRASSING PARTS!
"I BEGAN TO WONDER WHAT IT MIGHT SAY ON MY HEADSTONE. HEADSTONE?
"STONE! THAT'S IT!
"GREAT GRANDMA'S RING! THAT COULD BE MY TICKET OUT OF THIS SOGGY MESS!
"THE DIAMOND IN THE RING MADE A FIRST-CLASS GLASS CUTTER!
"NOW I WAS GOING TO PUT A STOP TO THEIR EVIL SCHEME ONCE AND FOR ALL!
THANKS FOR OFFERING TO TAKE ME FOR A RIDE IN YOUR HELICOPTER! YOU'RE A NICE GUY!
DON'T MENTION IT! I JUST BOUGHT A NEW ONE AND I'VE BEEN EAGER TO SHOW IT OFF!
"I RAN UP THE STAIRWAY TO THE ROOF. I FIGURED IF I COULD SABOTAGE THE HELICOPTER, I COULD STOP THEM IN THEIR TRACKS! BUT COULD I FINISH BEFORE THE BAD GUYS GOT THERE?

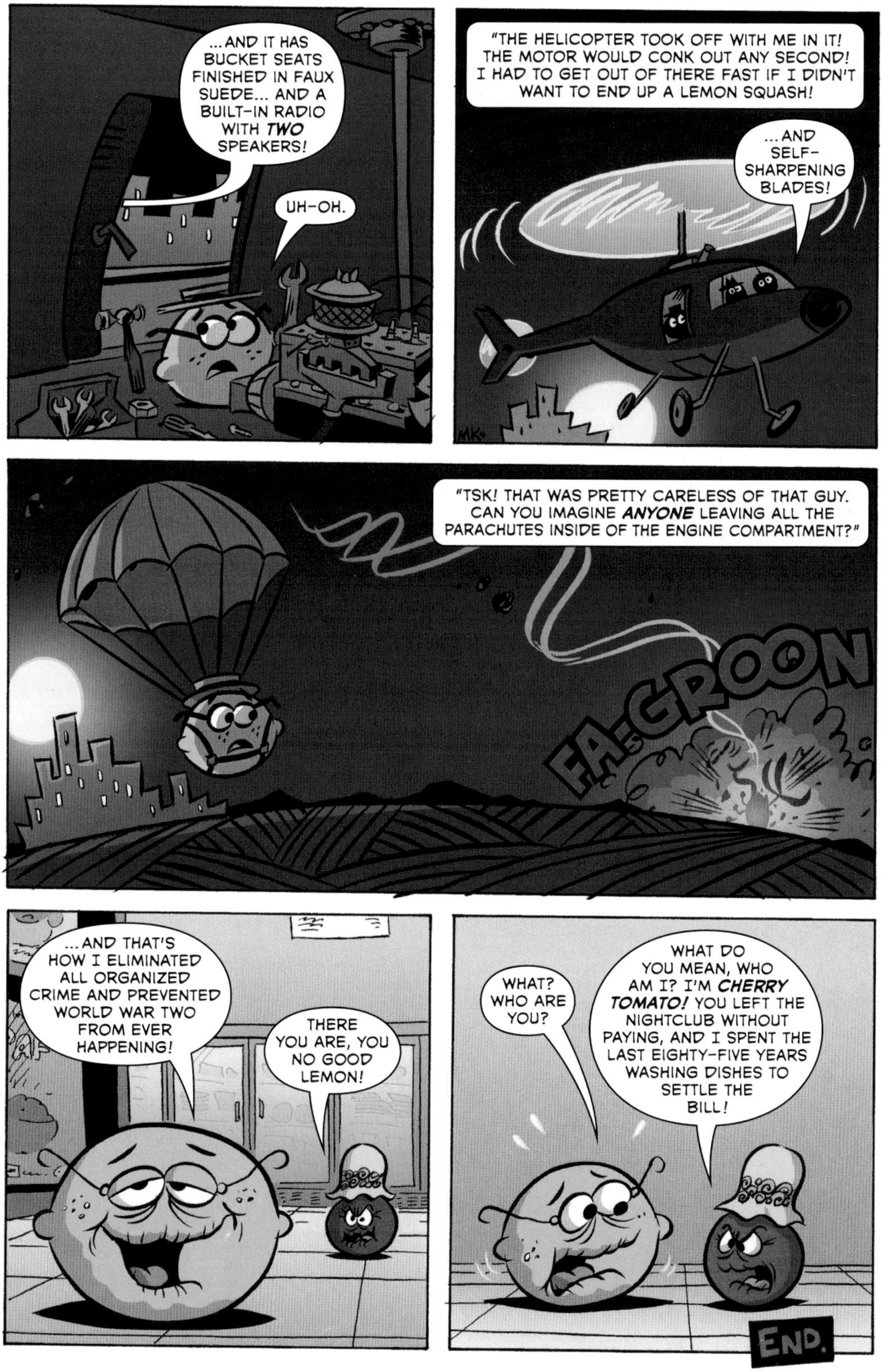
...AND IT HAS BUCKET SEATS FINISHED IN FAUX SUEDE... AND A BUILT-IN RADIO WITH *TWO* SPEAKERS!
UH-OH.
"THE HELICOPTER TOOK OFF WITH ME IN IT! THE MOTOR WOULD CONK OUT ANY SECOND! I HAD TO GET OUT OF THERE FAST IF I DIDN'T WANT TO END UP A LEMON SQUASH!
...AND SELF-SHARPENING BLADES!
"TSK! THAT WAS PRETTY CARELESS OF THAT GUY. CAN YOU IMAGINE *ANYONE* LEAVING ALL THE PARACHUTES INSIDE OF THE ENGINE COMPARTMENT?"
FA-GROON
...AND THAT'S HOW I ELIMINATED ALL ORGANIZED CRIME AND PREVENTED WORLD WAR TWO FROM EVER HAPPENING!
THERE YOU ARE, YOU NO GOOD LEMON!
WHAT? WHO ARE YOU?
WHAT DO YOU MEAN, WHO AM I? I'M *CHERRY TOMATO!* YOU LEFT THE NIGHTCLUB WITHOUT PAYING, AND I SPENT THE LAST EIGHTY-FIVE YEARS WASHING DISHES TO SETTLE THE BILL!
END.

A BEDTIME STORY

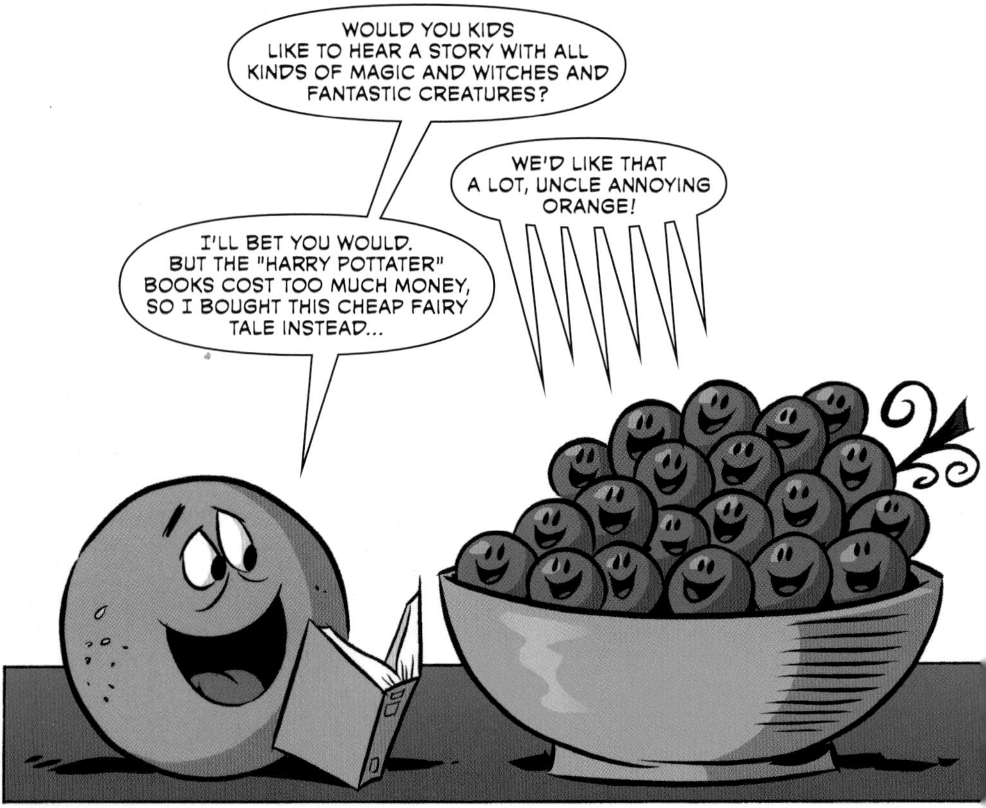
WOULD YOU KIDS LIKE TO HEAR A STORY WITH ALL KINDS OF MAGIC AND WITCHES AND FANTASTIC CREATURES?
WE'D LIKE THAT A LOT, UNCLE ANNOYING ORANGE!
I'LL BET YOU WOULD. BUT THE "HARRY POTTATER" BOOKS COST TOO MUCH MONEY, SO I BOUGHT THIS CHEAP FAIRY TALE INSTEAD...

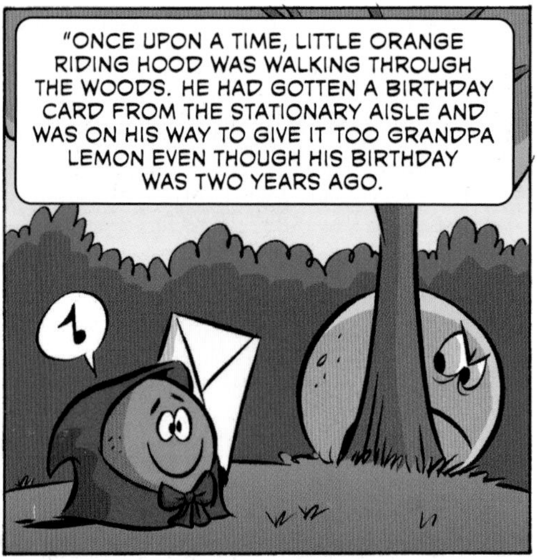
"ONCE UPON A TIME, LITTLE ORANGE RIDING HOOD WAS WALKING THROUGH THE WOODS. HE HAD GOTTEN A BIRTHDAY CARD FROM THE STATIONARY AISLE AND WAS ON HIS WAY TO GIVE IT TOO GRANDPA LEMON EVEN THOUGH HIS BIRTHDAY WAS TWO YEARS AGO.

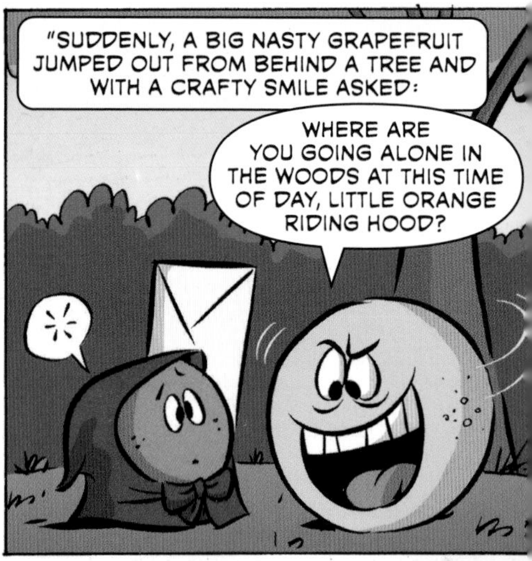
"SUDDENLY, A BIG NASTY GRAPEFRUIT JUMPED OUT FROM BEHIND A TREE AND WITH A CRAFTY SMILE ASKED:
WHERE ARE YOU GOING ALONE IN THE WOODS AT THIS TIME OF DAY, LITTLE ORANGE RIDING HOOD?

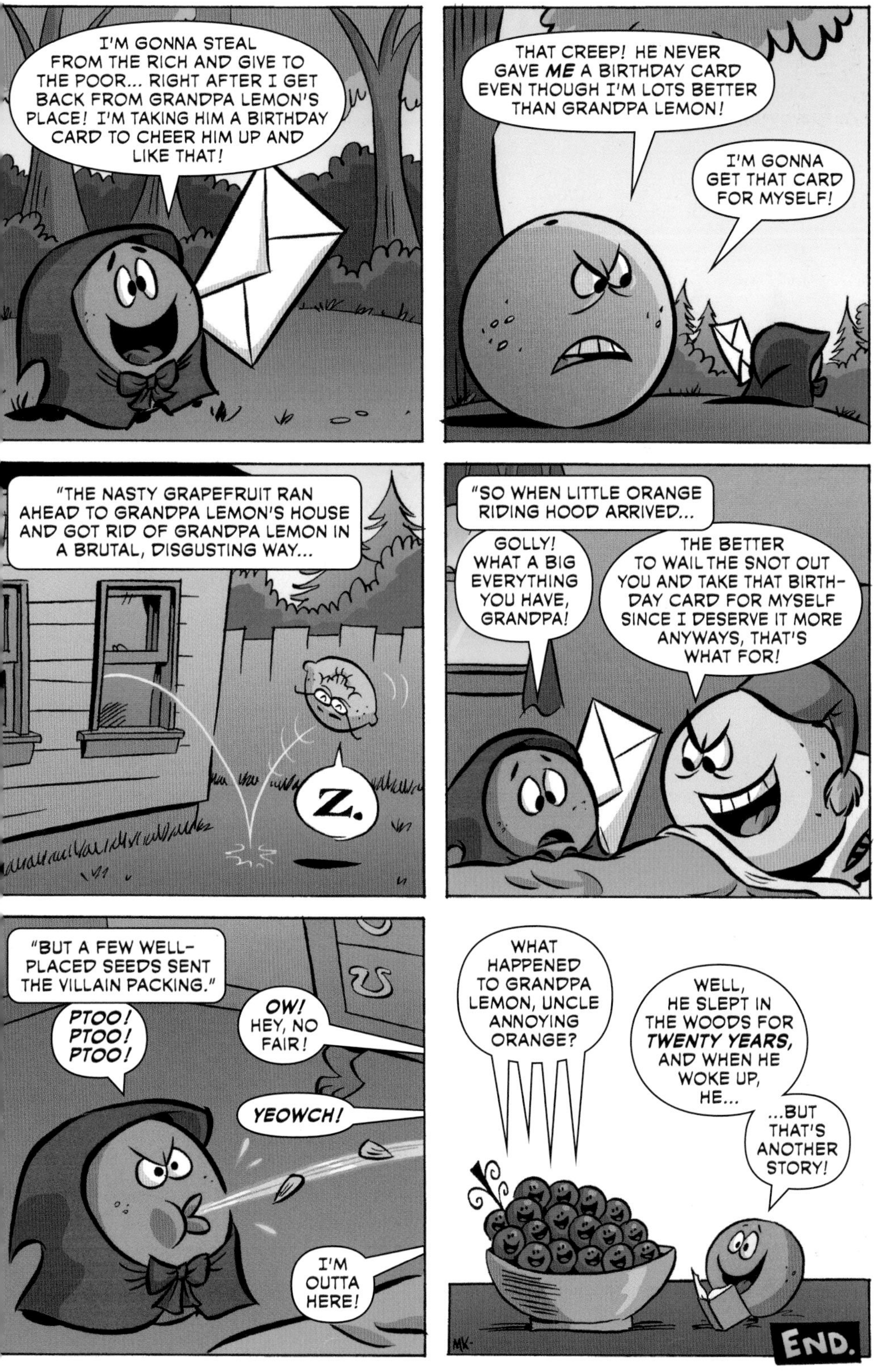
I'M GONNA STEAL FROM THE RICH AND GIVE TO THE POOR... RIGHT AFTER I GET BACK FROM GRANDPA LEMON'S PLACE! I'M TAKING HIM A BIRTHDAY CARD TO CHEER HIM UP AND LIKE THAT!
THAT CREEP! HE NEVER GAVE *ME* A BIRTHDAY CARD EVEN THOUGH I'M LOTS BETTER THAN GRANDPA LEMON!
I'M GONNA GET THAT CARD FOR MYSELF!
"THE NASTY GRAPEFRUIT RAN AHEAD TO GRANDPA LEMON'S HOUSE AND GOT RID OF GRANDPA LEMON IN A BRUTAL, DISGUSTING WAY...
Z.
"SO WHEN LITTLE ORANGE RIDING HOOD ARRIVED...
GOLLY! WHAT A BIG EVERYTHING YOU HAVE, GRANDPA!
THE BETTER TO WAIL THE SNOT OUT YOU AND TAKE THAT BIRTH-DAY CARD FOR MYSELF SINCE I DESERVE IT MORE ANYWAYS, THAT'S WHAT FOR!
"BUT A FEW WELL-PLACED SEEDS SENT THE VILLAIN PACKING."
PTOO! PTOO! PTOO!
OW! HEY, NO FAIR!
YEOWCH!
I'M OUTTA HERE!
WHAT HAPPENED TO GRANDPA LEMON, UNCLE ANNOYING ORANGE?
WELL, HE SLEPT IN THE WOODS FOR *TWENTY YEARS,* AND WHEN HE WOKE UP, HE...
...BUT THAT'S ANOTHER STORY!
END.

WATCH OUT FOR PAPERCUTZ™

Welcome to the fantastic, fruit-filled first ANNOYING ORANGE™ graphic novel from PAPERCUTZ. We're the folks dedicated to publishing great graphic novels for all ages. I'm your annoying Editor-in-Chief, Jim Salicrup, here to offer a little behind-the-scenes info on the making of this sure-to-be-a-valuable collectors' item graphic novel.

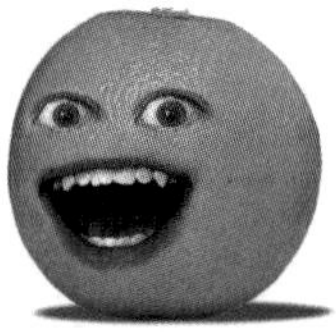

Of course, it all started with Dane Boedigheimer, the goofball filmmaker* who created the transmedia sensation known as ANNOYING ORANGE. Even though Daneboe brings forth new ANNOYING ORANGE videos on a fairly regular basis on YouTube, there is still a vast hunger for more Orange! Even with an all-new TV series on the CARTOON NETWORK, Orange fans remain unsatisfied. It is at this point, sensing the pent-up yearning for more ANNOYING ORANGE that Papercutz so unselfishly agreed to publish an all-new series of ANNOYING ORANGE graphic novels! Even though we're convinced that even this comicbook incarnation will only continue to create even more demand for more, more, and even MORE ANNOYING ORANGE! At this point it's merely a matter of time before you'll soon be bombarded with ANNOYING ORANGE: The Motion Picture, followed by the inevitable ANNOYING ORANGE: the Broadway Musical, and much, much more!

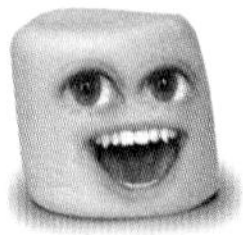

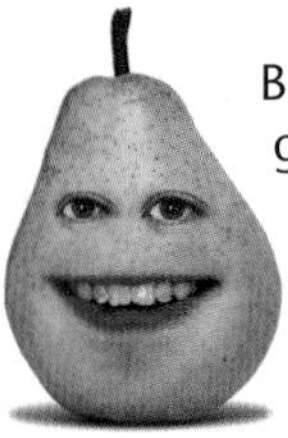

But until then we sincerely hope you'll enjoy the ANNOYING ORANGE graphic novel series! Created under Daneboe's ever-watchful two left eyes, and written and drawn by two contributing cartoonists to the TV series, Mike Kazaleh and Scott Shaw! (Yeah, the exclamation point is part of his name…), we're confident we can deliver that FRESH SQUEEZED COMEDY™ that you love so much!

In fact, to attempt to satisfy your curiosity concerning the mystery men responsible for all this, we present on the following pages, brief biographical essays on Daneboe, Scott, and Mike (Mystery women Laurie E. Smith and Jayjay Jackson will have to remain a mystery… for now). And like all things concerning ANNOYING ORANGE, I'm sure all this will simply leave you wanting more, more, and even MORE. So, just because we kinda like you, we'll be back in just a few short months with just that—more, more and even MORE with ANNOYING ORANGE #2 "Orange You Glad You're Not Me?" You're an apple if you miss it!

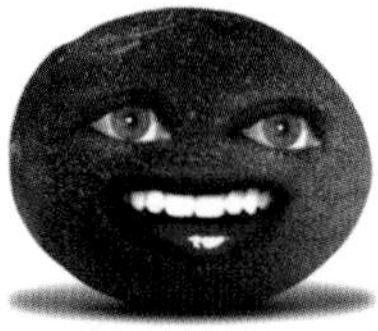

JIM

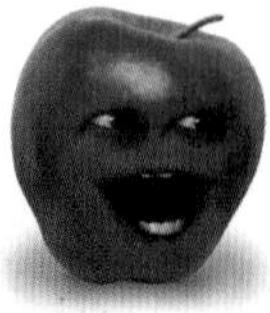

STAY IN TOUCH!

EMAIL:	papercutz@papercutz.com
WEB:	www.papercutz.com
TWITTER:	@papercutzgn
FACEBOOK:	PAPERCUTZGRAPHICNOVELS
REGULAR MAIL:	Papercutz, 160 Broadway, Suite 700, East Wing, New York, NY 10038

*Hey, that's what he calls himself! See for yourself on the very next page!

DANE BOEDIGHEIMER

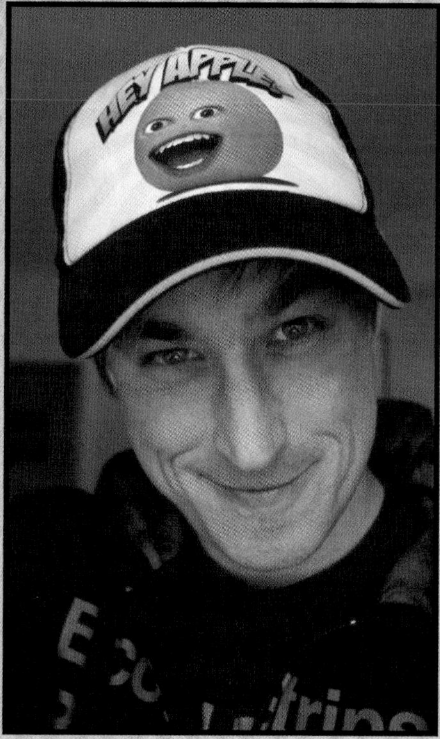
HEY APPLE!

Dane (or Daneboe as he's known online) is a filmmaker and goofball extraordinaire. Dane spent most of his life in the glamorous Midwest, Harwood, North Dakota, to be exact. With nothing better to do, (it was North Dakota) at around the age of twelve, Dane began making short movies and videos with his parents' camcorder. Since then he has made hundreds, if not thousands of short web videos... many of which are only funny to him. But Dane has remained determined to make "the perfect short comedy film;" one that will end all social problems and bring laughter to all the children of the world.

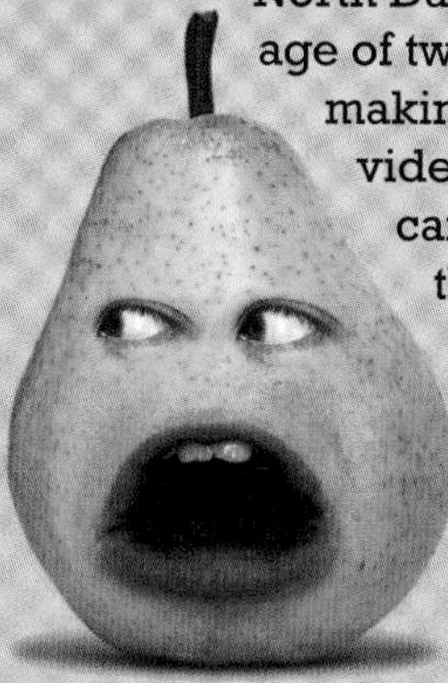

Currently, Dane is most widely known for creating ANNOYING ORANGE one of the most successful web series ever. Orange has over 2.4 million subscribers on YouTube, 10 million facebook fans, and has over 1.1 billion video views total. On top of that, the Annoying Orange series premiered on CARTOON NETWORK boasting the #1 telecast of the day among boys 6-11 and has a complete line of toys, shirts, and other merchandise currently in JCPenney & Toys"R"Us amongst other major retailers.

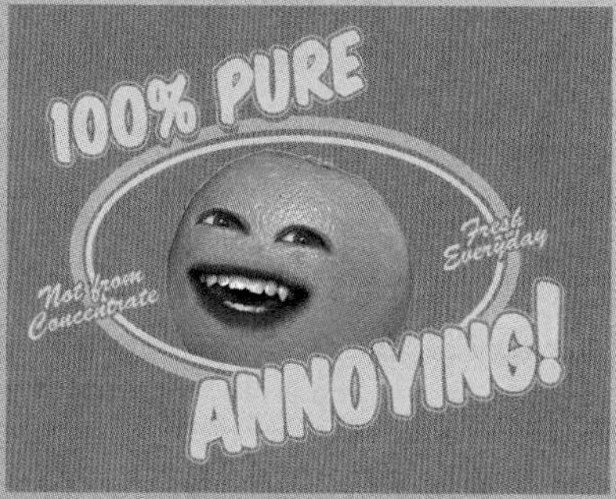
100% PURE
Not from Concentrate
Fresh Everyday
ANNOYING!

Not to be completely undone, Dane's other videos have been viewed over 650 million times and have been featured on TV, as well as some of the most popular entertainment, news, and video sharing sites on the Internet.

In Dane's downtime he enjoys... oh, who are we kidding? Dane doesn't have any downtime. He wouldn't know what to do with himself if he did.

SPENCER GROVE

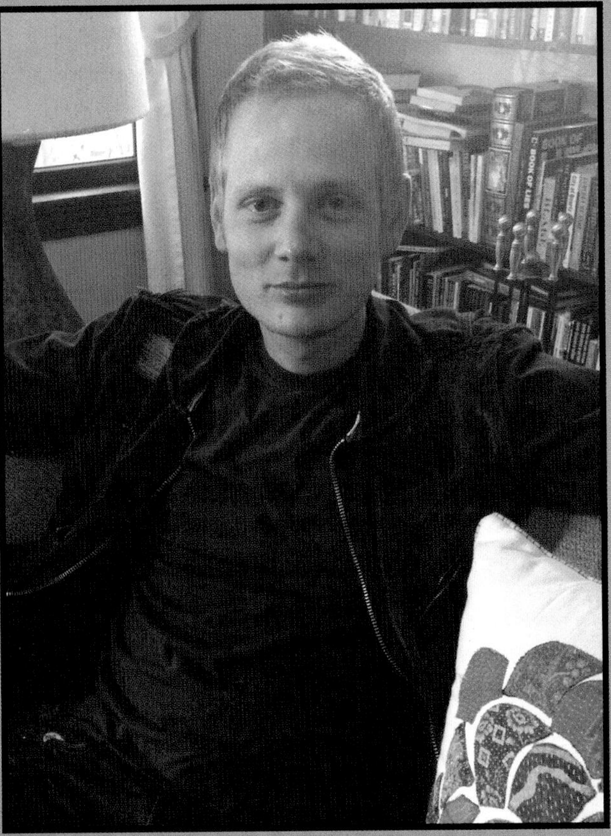

Spencer Grove has written plays, prose, television scripts and more online videos than any sane person should attempt. Also, he bakes a mean apple pie.

He began his career in independent productions, working on everything from infomercials to award shows, eventually moving to MTV where he served as an Associate Producer on Pimp My Ride. Since 2009, he has served as the head writer of the Annoying Orange web series, creating and co-creating the supporting cast and developing the ever-expanding online world of the Orange.

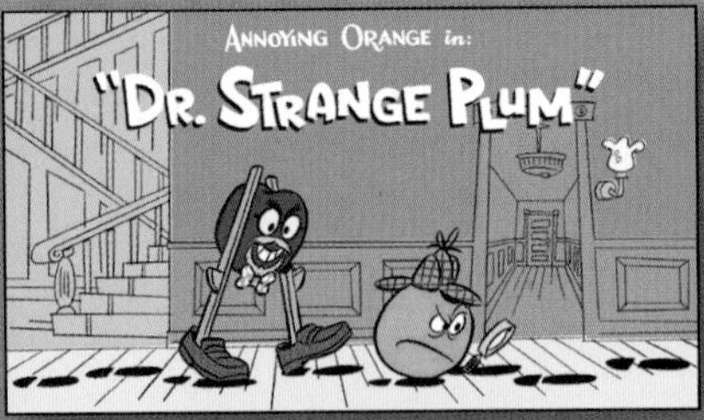
Annoying Orange in:
"Dr. Strange Plum"

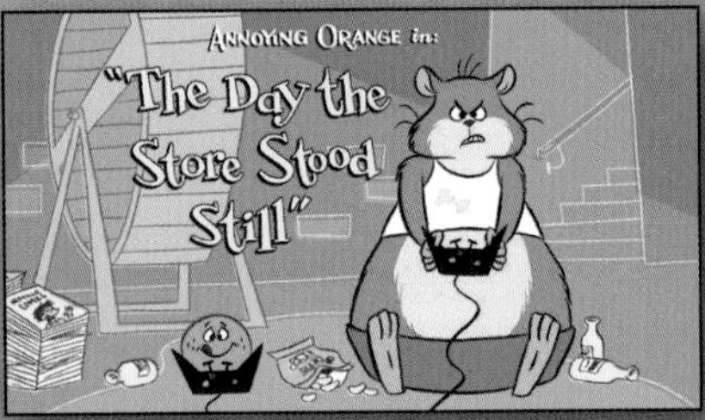
Annoying Orange in:
"The Day the Store Stood Still"

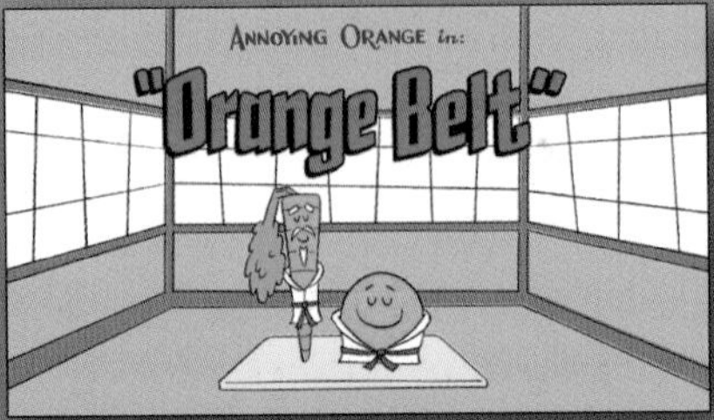
Annoying Orange in:
"Orange Belt"

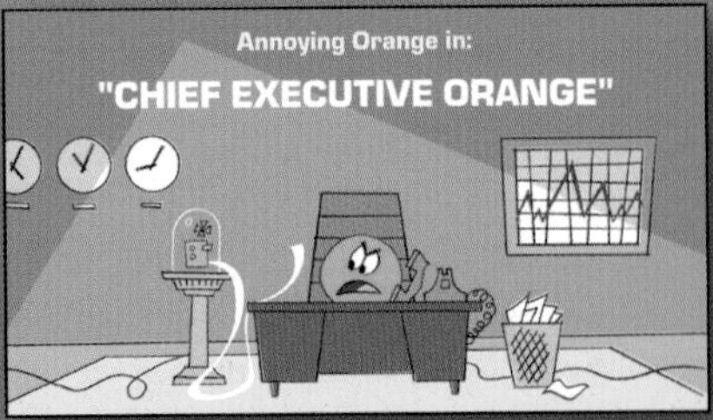
Annoying Orange in:
"CHIEF EXECUTIVE ORANGE"

SCOTT SHAW!

Scott Shaw! is an example of Hunter S. Thompson's statement: "When the going gets weird, the weird turn pro." An award-winning cartoonist/writer of comicbooks, animation, advertising and toy design, Scott is also a historian of all forms of cartooning. After writing and drawing a number of underground "comix," Scott has worked on many mainstream comicbooks, including: SONIC THE HEDGEHOG (Archie); SIMPSONS COMICS, BART SIMPSON'S TREEHOUSE OF HORROR and RADIOACTIVE MAN (Bongo); WEIRD TALES OF THE RAMONES (Rhino); and his co-creation with Roy Thomas, CAPTAIN CARROT AND HIS AMAZING ZOO CREW! (DC). Scott has also worked on numerous animated cartoons, including: producing/directing of John Candy's Camp Candy (NBC/DIC/Saban) and Martin Short's The Completely Mental Misadventures of Ed Grimley (NBC/Hanna-Barbera Productions); Garfield and Friends (CBS/Film Roman); and the Emmy-winning Jim Henson's Muppet Babies (CBS/Marvel Productions).

Above an example of Scott's storyboards for the ANNOYING ORANGE TV series

As Senior Art Director for the Ogilvy & Mather advertising agency, Scott worked on dozens of commercials for Post Pebbles cereals with the Flintstones. He also designed a line of Hanna-Barbera action figures for McFarlane Toys. Scott was one of the comic fans who organized the first San Diego Comic-Con, where he has become known for performing his hilarious ODDBALL COMICS slide show. www.shawcartoons.com. Scott is also a gag man and storyboard cartoonist on Cartoon Network's ANNOYING ORANGE program. His favorite fruit is forbidden.

MIKE KAZALEH

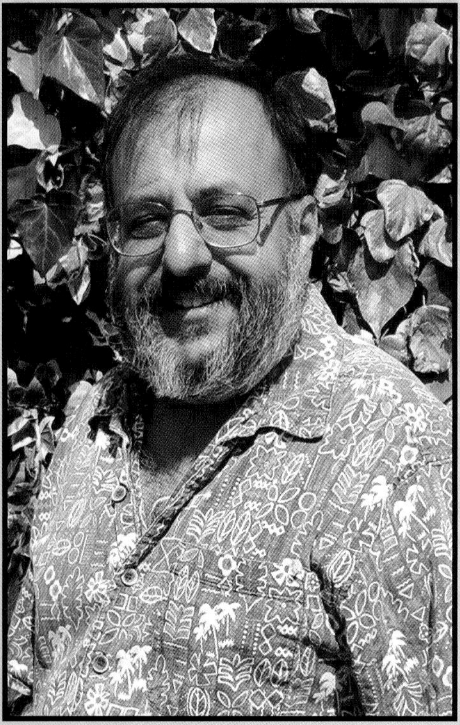

Mike Kazaleh is a veteran of comicbooks and animated cartoons. He began his career producing low budget commercials and sales films out of his tiny studio in Detroit, Michigan. Mike soon moved to Los Angeles, California and since then he has worked for most of the major cartoon studios and comicbook companies.

He has worked with such characters as The Flintstones, The Simpsons, Mighty Mouse, Krypto the Superdog, Ren and Stimpy, Cow and Chicken, and Bugs Bunny, as well as creating his own independent comics including THE ADVENTURES OF CAPTAIN JACK. Before all this stuff happened, Mike was a TV repairman.

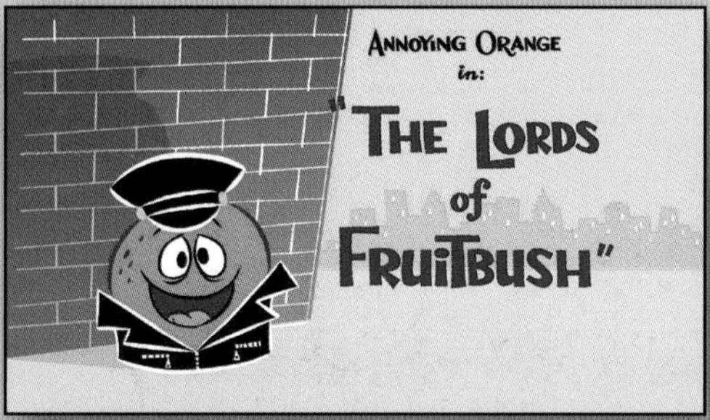
ANNOYING ORANGE in:
"THE LORDS of FRUITBUSH"

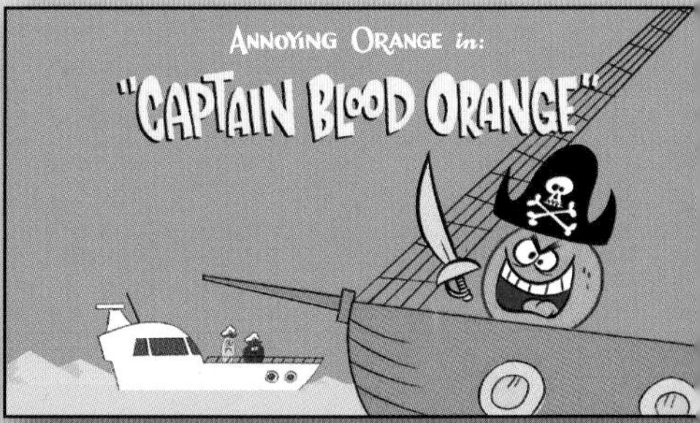
ANNOYING ORANGE in:
"CAPTAIN BLOOD ORANGE"

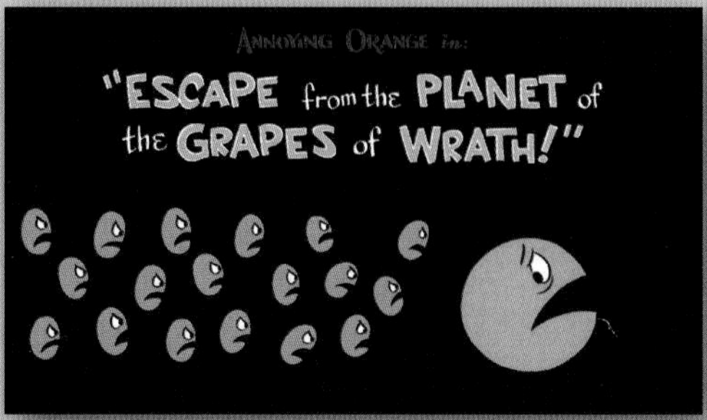
ANNOYING ORANGE in:
"ESCAPE from the PLANET of the GRAPES of WRATH!"

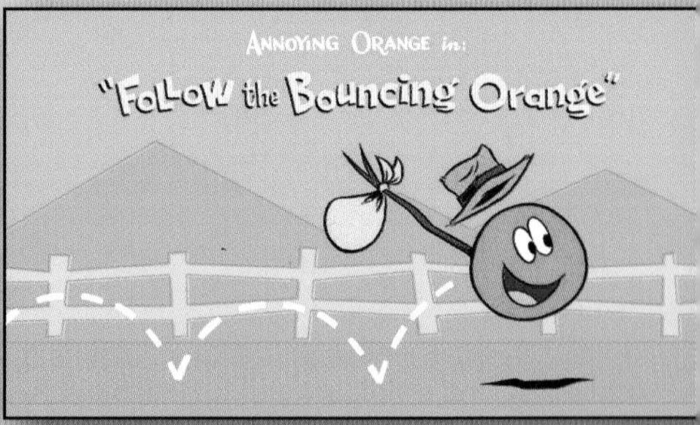
ANNOYING ORANGE in:
"Follow the Bouncing Orange"

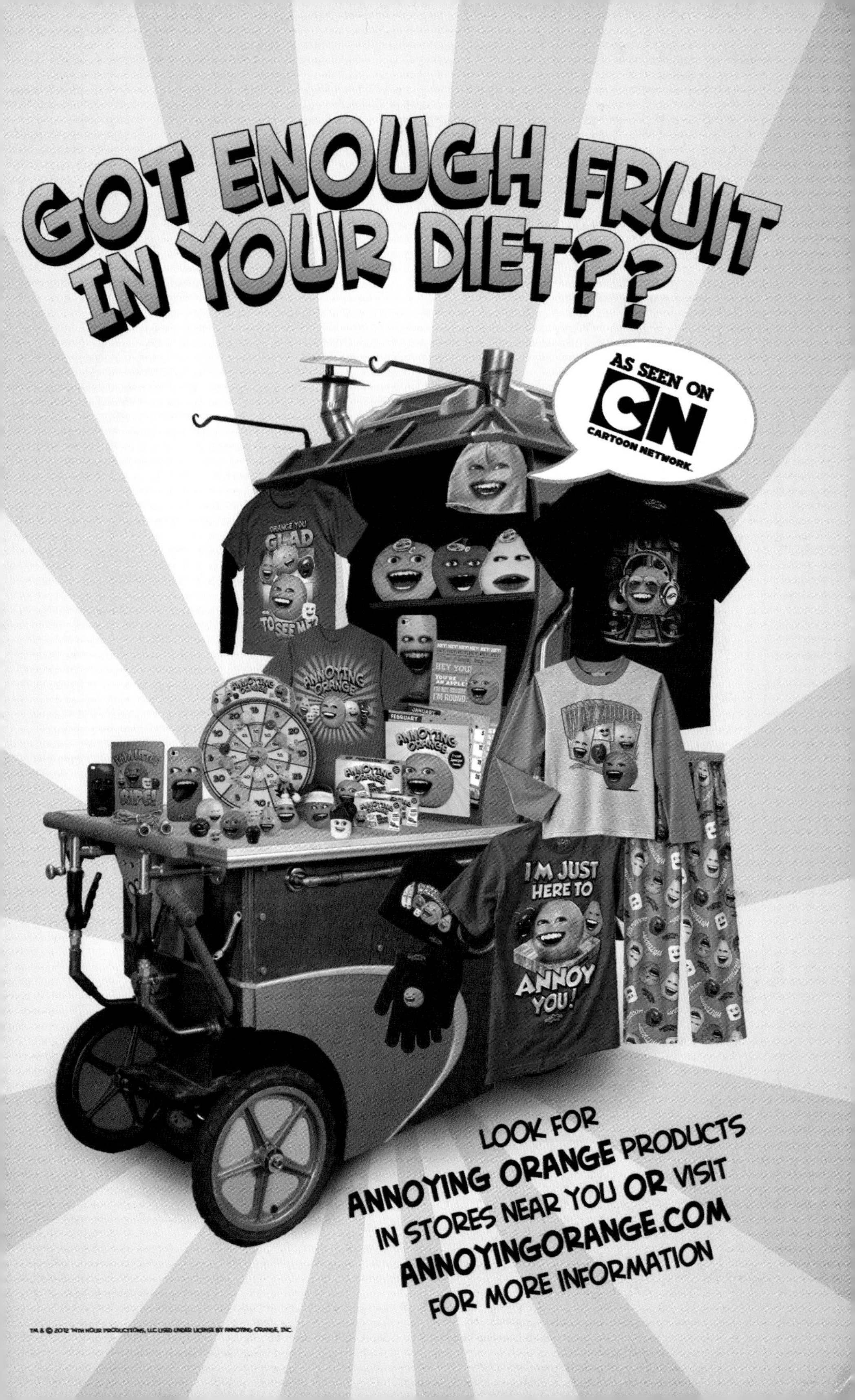
GOT ENOUGH FRUIT IN YOUR DIET??
AS SEEN ON
CN
CARTOON NETWORK
ORANGE YOU GLAD TO SEE ME?
ANNOYING ORANGE
HEY YOU!
I'M JUST HERE TO ANNOY YOU!
LOOK FOR
ANNOYING ORANGE PRODUCTS
IN STORES NEAR YOU OR VISIT
ANNOYINGORANGE.COM
FOR MORE INFORMATION

SOME EXCITING SCENES FROM OUR NEXT GRAPHIC NOVEL!

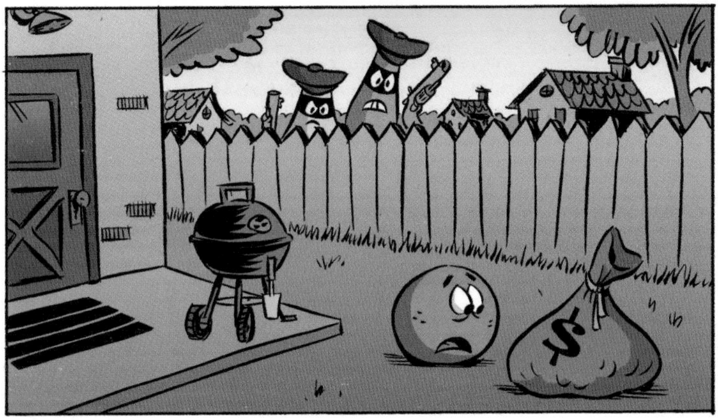

ORANGE, THE FAMOUS WORLD WAR I FLYING ACE GETS SHOT DOWN BEHIND ENEMY LINES. THERE HE FINDS THAT THE LUFTWAFFE HAS INVENTED A NEW SECRET DIRIGIBLE THAT COULD WIN THE WAR. CAN ORANGE DESTROY THE BLIMP AND GET BACK TO HIS OWN SQUADRON IN TIME?

THERE IS A DROUGHT ON THE ORANGE FARM AND THINGS LOOK DIRE. IF GLUEPOT, THE FAMILY HORSE CAN WIN THE PENNSYLTUCKY DERBY, THEY COULD USE THE PRIZE MONEY TO BUY IRRIGATION EQUIPMENT. UNFORTUNATELY THE EVIL COLONEL QUINCE HAS ENTERED HIS HORSE IN THE CONTEST, AND HE WANTS GLUEPOT TO FAIL SO HE CAN BUY THE ORANGE FARM FOR PENNIES ON THE DOLLAR.

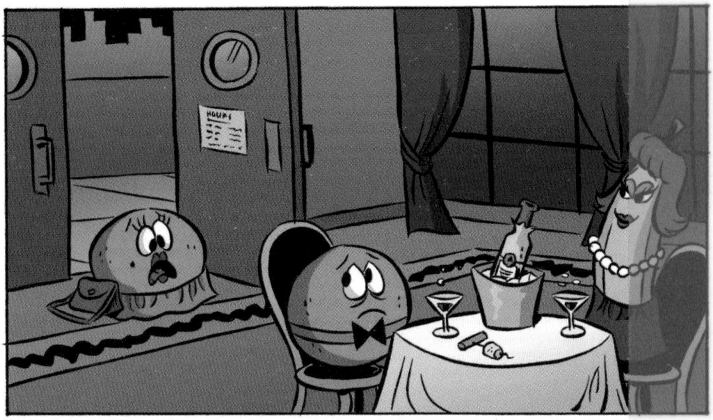

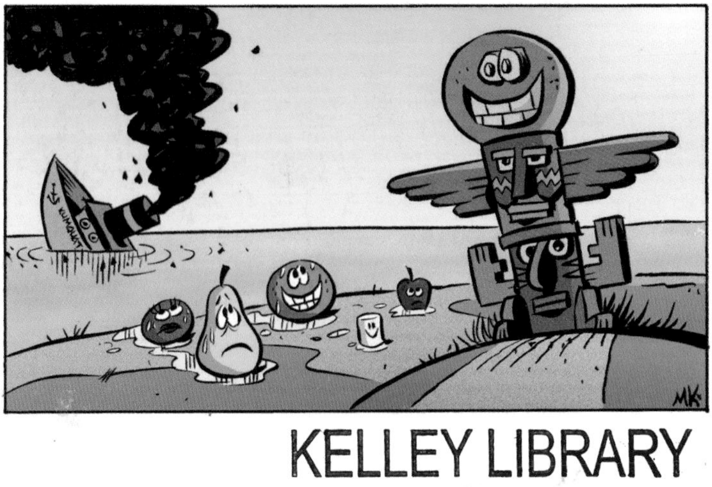
MK

ASTRONAUT ORANGE ATTEMPTS TO BE THE FIRST FRUIT TO ORBIT THE PLANET JUPITER. THE FANTASTIC SPEED OF THE EXPERIMENTAL ROCKET HURLS HIM BACK IN TIME AND HE FINDS HIMSELF TRAPPED IN A WORLD OF PRIMORDIAL PRODUCE. THIS DISCOVERY WOULD BE A GREAT BOON TO SCIENCE IF ONLY ORANGE CAN SURVIVE AND RETURN TO HIS OWN TIME WHICH ISN'T ANY TOO LIKELY REALLY.